Neil Gaiman has written highly acclaimed books for both children and adults and is the first author to have won the Carnegie and Newbery Medals for the same work – *The Graveyard Book*. Many of his books, including *Coraline* and *Stardust*, have been made into films; *Neverwhere* has been adapted for TV and radio; and *American Gods* and *Good Omens* have been adapted into major TV series. He has also written two amazing episodes of *Doctor Who* and appeared in *The Simpsons* as himself.

BOOKS BY NEIL GAIMAN FROM BLOOMSBURY

NOVELS

Illustrated by Chris Riddell
Coraline
Fortunately, the Milk ...
The Graveyard Book
Odd and the Frost Giants
The Sleeper and the Spindle

Norse Mythology

SHORT STORIES

M Is for Magic

PICTURE BOOKS

Illustrated by Dave McKean
Crazy Hair
The Day I Swapped My Dad for Two Goldfish
The Wolves in the Walls

Illustrated by Charles Vess
Blueberry Girl
Instructions

Illustrated by Gris Grimly
The Dangerous Alphabet

Illustrated by Adam Rex
Chu's Day
Chu's Day at the Beach
Chu's First Day at School

Illustrated by Divya Srinivasan
Cinnamon

GRAPHIC NOVELS

Illustrated by Dave McKean
Signal to Noise
The Comical Tragedy or Tragical Comedy of Mr Punch
MirrorMask

Illustrated by P. Craig Russell
Coraline
The Graveyard Book: Volume One
The Graveyard Book: Volume Two

NEIL GAIMAN
Coraline

ILLUSTRATED BY
Chris Riddell

BLOOMSBURY
LONDON OXFORD NEW YORK NEW DELHI SYDNEY

Bloomsbury Publishing, London, Oxford, New York, New Delhi and Sydney

First published in Great Britain in 2002 by Bloomsbury Publishing Plc
50 Bedford Square, London WC1B 3DP

www.bloomsbury.com
www.neilgaiman.com

This edition published in October 2013

A CIP catalogue record for this book is available from the British Library

ISBN 978 1 4088 4175 4

Typeset by Hewer Text UK Ltd, Edinburgh
Printed and bound by CPI Group (UK) Ltd, Croydon CR0 4YY

20

To be kept up to date about our authors and books,
please visit www.bloomsbury.com/newsletters and sign up
for our newsletters, including news about Neil Gaiman.

I started this for Holly
I finished it for Maddy

*Fairy tales are more than true: not because
they tell us that dragons exist, but because
they tell us that dragons can be beaten.*

G.K. Chesterton

INTRODUCTION

We moved into our flat in Littlemead, in the tiny Sussex town of Nutley, in the south of England, in 1987. Once upon a time it had been a manor house, built for the physician to the King of England himself, so I was told by the old man who had once owned the house (before he sold it to a pair of local builders). It had been a very grand house then, but it was now converted into flats.

Flat number 4, where we lived, was a good place, if a little odd. Above us, a Greek family. Beneath us, a little old lady, half blind, who would telephone me whenever my little children moved, and tell me that she was not certain what was happening upstairs, but she thought that there were elephants. I was never entirely sure how many flats there were in the house, nor how many of them were occupied.

We had a hallway running the length of the flat, as big as any room. At the end of the hall hung a wardrobe door, as a mirror.

When I started to write a book for Holly, my five-year-old daughter, I set it in the house. It seemed easy. That way I wouldn't have to explain to her where anything was. I changed a couple of things, of course, swapped the position of Holly's bedroom and the lounge.

Then I took a closed oak-panelled door that opened on to a brick wall, and a sense of place, from the drawing room in the house I grew up in.

That house was big and old, and it had been split in two just before we moved there. We had the servants' quarters and the oak-panelled drawing room ('Only for best') with a door at the end that had once been the family's entrance, but that now led nowhere. It opened on to a brick wall.

I took that room and that door, along with the front room of my grandmother's house ('Only for best, not for the family', still-life oil paintings of fruit on the walls) and I put them into the book I had started writing.

The book was called *Coraline*. I had typed the name Caroline, and it came out wrong. I looked at the word 'Coraline' and knew it was someone's name. I wanted to know what happened to her.

Holly liked scary stories, with witches and brave little girls in them. Those were the kinds of stories she told me. So Holly's story was going to be scary.

I wrote an opening that I later deleted. It went:

This is the story of Coraline, who was small for her age, and found herself in darkest danger. Before it was all over Coraline had seen what lay behind mirrors, and had a close call with a bad hand, and had come face to face with her other mother; she had rescued her true parents from a fate worse than death and triumphed against overwhelming odds.

This is the story of Coraline, who lost her parents, and found them again, and (more or less) escaped (more or less) unscathed.

I stopped writing Holly's book when we moved to America. (I had been writing it in my own time. It didn't seem like I had any 'own time' any longer.)

Six years later I picked it up and continued from the middle of the sentence I'd stopped at in August 1992.

It was:

'Hello,' said Coraline. 'How did you get in?' The cat didn't say anything. Coraline got out of bed

I started it again because I realised that if I didn't, my youngest daughter, Maddy, would be too old for it by the time I was done. I started it for Holly. I finished it for Maddy.

We were living in a gothic old house in the middle of America, with a turret and a wraparound porch with steps up to it. It's a house built over a hundred years ago by a German immigrant – a cartographer (that's someone who makes maps) and artist. His son, Henry, was said to have been the first man to put an engine on a boat, or on a bicycle, and was described as 'the greatest creative figure in the history of the racing car'.

Now I was writing *Coraline* again, I still had no time, so I would write fifty words a night in bed, before I fell asleep. I went on a cruise to raise money for the First Amendment (that's the one about Freedom of Speech) in comics, and wrote more of the story sitting out on the deck. I finished it in a little cabin on a lake in the woods.

Dave McKean, artist and friend, took photographs of Littlemead, which he then played with to make the house on the back cover of the original American edition.

When Henry Selick made his stop-motion animated film of *Coraline*, he invited me to the studio. There were a lot of sets there, each behind a black curtain. Henry proudly showed me the house that Coraline lived in in the film. She'd moved from somewhere in England to Oregon now, and the house she was in was called The Pink Palace.

'That's my house,' I told Henry.

And it was. Henry Selick's Pink Palace was the house I live in now, turret and porch and all. None of us are quite sure how that happened. But it seemed strangely appropriate for a book that was started for one daughter in one house and finished for another in another house.

The book was published in 2002, and people liked it. It won awards. More importantly than that, it worked, at least for some people.

I'd wanted to write a story for my daughters that told them something I wished I'd known when I was a boy: that being brave doesn't mean you aren't scared. Being brave means you are scared, really scared, badly scared, and you do the right thing anyway.

So now, ten years later, I've started running into women who tell me that *Coraline* got them through hard times in their lives. That when they were scared they thought of Coraline, and they did the right thing anyway.

And that, more than anything, makes it all worthwhile.

Chris Riddell has done a new set of illustrations for this tenth anniversary edition. I looked at the picture he had done for the cover and was amazed and delighted by the way that he had combined both of the houses – the one I live in now, the one I lived in then.

Neil Gaiman

Coraline, who was standing in the doorway,
cast a huge and distorted shadow . . .

CHAPTER 1

Coraline discovered the door a little while after they moved into the house.

It was a very old house – it had an attic under the roof and a cellar under the ground and an overgrown garden with huge old trees in it.

Coraline's family didn't own all of the house, it was too big for that. Instead they owned part of it.

There were other people who lived in the old house.

Miss Spink and Miss Forcible lived in the flat below Coraline's, on the ground floor. They were both old and round, and they lived in their flat with a number of ageing Highland terriers who had names like Hamish and Andrew and Jock. Once upon a time Miss Spink and Miss Forcible had been actresses, as Miss Spink told Coraline the first time she met her.

'You see, Caroline,' Miss Spink said, getting Coraline's name wrong, 'both myself and Miss Forcible were famous actresses, in our time. We trod the boards, lovey. Oh, don't let Hamish eat the fruitcake, or he'll be up all night with his tummy.'

'It's Coraline. Not Caroline. Coraline,' said Coraline.

In the flat above Coraline's, under the roof, was a crazy old man with a big moustache. He told Coraline that he was training a mouse circus. He wouldn't let anyone see it.

'One day, little Caroline, when they are all ready, everyone in the whole world will see the wonders of my mouse circus. You ask me why you cannot see it now. Is that what you asked me?'

'No,' said Coraline quietly, 'I asked you not to call me Caroline. It's Coraline.'

'The reason you cannot see the mouse circus,' said the man upstairs, 'is that the mice are not yet ready and rehearsed. Also, they refuse to play the songs I have written for them. All the songs I have written for the mice to play go *oompah oompah*. But the white mice will only play *toodle oodle*, like that. I am thinking of trying them on different types of cheese.'

Coraline didn't think there really was a mouse circus. She thought the old man was probably making it up.

The day after they moved in, Coraline went exploring.

She explored the garden. It was a big garden: at the very back was an old tennis court, but no one in the house played tennis and the fence around the court had holes in it and the net had mostly rotted away; there was an old rose garden, filled with stunted, flyblown rose bushes; there was a rockery that was all rocks; there was a fairy ring, made of squidgy brown toadstools which smelled dreadful if you accidentally trod on them.

There was also a well. On the first day Coraline's family moved in, Miss Spink and Miss Forcible made a point of telling Coraline how dangerous the well was, and they warned her to be sure she kept away from it. So Coraline set off to explore for it, so that she knew where it was, to keep away from it properly.

She found it on the third day, in an overgrown meadow beside the tennis court, behind a clump of trees – a low brick circle almost hidden in the high grass. The well had been covered over by wooden boards, to stop anyone falling in. There was a small knothole in one of the boards, and Coraline spent an afternoon dropping pebbles and acorns through the hole, and waiting, and counting, until she heard the *plop* as they hit the water, far below.

Coraline also explored for animals. She found a hedgehog, and a snakeskin (but no snake), and a rock that looked just like a frog, and a toad that looked just like a rock.

There was also a haughty black cat, who would sit on walls and tree stumps and watch her, but would slip away if ever she went over to try to play with it.

That was how she spent her first two weeks at the house – exploring the garden and the grounds.

Her mother made her come back inside for dinner and for lunch; and Coraline had to make sure she dressed up warmly before she went out, for it was a very cold summer that year; but go out she did, exploring, every day until the day it rained, when Coraline had to stay inside.

'What should I do?' asked Coraline.

'Read a book,' said her mother. 'Watch a video. Play with your toys. Go and pester Miss Spink or Miss Forcible, or the crazy old man upstairs.'

'No,' said Coraline. 'I don't want to do those things. I want to explore.'

'I don't really mind what you do,' said Coraline's mother, 'as long as you don't make a mess.'

Coraline went over to the window and watched the rain come down. It wasn't the kind of rain you could go out in, it was the other kind, the kind that threw itself down from the sky and splashed where it landed. It was rain that meant business, and currently its business was turning the garden into a muddy, wet soup.

Coraline had watched all the videos. She was bored with her toys, and she'd read all her books.

She turned on the television. She went from channel to channel to channel, but there was nothing on but men in suits talking about the stock market, and sports programmes. Eventually, she found something to watch: it was the last half of a natural-history programme about something called protective coloration. She watched animals, birds and insects which disguised themselves as leaves or twigs or other animals to escape from things that could hurt them. She enjoyed it, but it ended too soon, and was followed by a programme about a cake factory.

It was time to talk to her father.

Coraline's father was home. Both of her parents worked, doing things on computers, which meant that they were home a lot of the time. Each of them had their own study.

'Hello, Coraline,' he said when she came in, without turning round.

'Mmph,' said Coraline. 'It's raining.'

'Yup,' said her father. 'It's bucketing down.'

'No,' said Coraline, 'it's just raining. Can I go outside?'

'What does your mother say?'

'She says, "You're not going out in weather like that, Coraline Jones".'

'Then, no.'

'But I want to carry on exploring.'

'Then explore the flat,' suggested her father. 'Look – here's a piece of paper and a pen. Count all the doors and windows. List everything blue. Mount an expedition to discover the hot-water tank. And leave me alone to work.'

'Can I go into the drawing room?' The drawing room was where the Joneses kept the expensive (and uncomfortable) furniture Coraline's grand-mother had left them when she died. Coraline wasn't allowed in there. Nobody went in there. It was only for best.

'If you don't make a mess. And you don't touch anything.'

Coraline considered this carefully, then she

took the paper and pen and went off to explore the inside of the flat.

She discovered the hot-water tank (it was in a cupboard in the kitchen).

She counted everything blue (153).

She counted the windows (21).

She counted the doors (14).

Of the doors that she found, thirteen opened and closed. The other, the big, carved, brown wooden door at the far corner of the drawing room, was locked.

She said to her mother, 'Where does that door go?'

'Nowhere, dear.'

'It has to go somewhere.'

Her mother shook her head. 'Look,' she told Coraline.

She reached up, and took a string of keys from the top of the kitchen doorframe. She sorted through them carefully and selected the oldest, biggest, blackest, rustiest key. They went into the drawing room. She unlocked the door with the key.

The door swung open.

Her mother was right. The door didn't go anywhere. It opened on to a brick wall.

'When this place was just one house,' said Coraline's mother, 'that door went somewhere.

When they turned the house into flats, they simply bricked it up. The other side is the empty flat on the other side of the house, the one that's still for sale.'

She shut the door and put the string of keys back on top of the kitchen doorframe.

'You didn't lock it,' said Coraline.

Her mother shrugged. 'Why should I lock it?' she asked. 'It doesn't go anywhere.'

Coraline didn't say anything.

It was nearly dark now, and the rain was still coming down, pattering against the windows and blurring the lights of the cars in the street outside.

Coraline's father stopped working and made them all dinner.

Coraline was disgusted. 'Daddy,' she said, 'you've made a *recipe* again.'

'It's leek and potato stew, with a tarragon garnish and melted Gruyère cheese,' he admitted.

Coraline sighed. Then she went to the freezer and got out some microwave chips and a microwave mini-pizza.

'You know I don't like recipes,' she told her father, while her dinner went round and round and the little red numbers on the microwave oven counted down to zero.

'If you tried it, maybe you'd like it,' said Coraline's father, but she shook her head.

That night, Coraline lay awake in her bed. The rain had stopped, and she was almost asleep when something went *t-t-t-t-t-t*. She sat up in bed.

Something went *kreeee* . . .

. . . *aaaak*.

Coraline got out of bed and looked down the hall, but saw nothing strange. She walked down the hallway. From her parents' bedroom came a low snoring – that was her father – and an occasional sleeping mutter – that was her mother.

Coraline wondered if she'd dreamed it, whatever it was.

Something moved.

It was little more than a shadow, and it scuttled down the darkened hall fast, like a little patch of night.

She hoped it wasn't a spider. Spiders made Coraline intensely uncomfortable.

The black shape went into the drawing room and Coraline followed it in, a little nervously.

The room was dark. The only light came from the hall, and Coraline, who was standing in the doorway, cast a huge and distorted shadow on to the drawing-room carpet: she looked like a thin giant woman.

Coraline was just wondering whether or not she ought to turn on the light when she saw the black shape edge slowly out from beneath the sofa. It paused, and then dashed silently across the carpet towards the farthest corner of the room.

There was no furniture in that corner of the room.

Coraline turned on the light.

There was nothing in the corner. Nothing but the old door that opened on to the brick wall.

She was sure that her mother had shut the door, but now it was ever so slightly open. Just a crack. Coraline went over to it and looked in. There was nothing there – just a wall, built of red bricks.

Coraline closed the old wooden door, turned out the light, and went back to bed.

She dreamed of black shapes that slid from place to place, avoiding the light, until they were all gathered together under the moon. Little black shapes with little red eyes and sharp yellow teeth.

They started to sing:

> *We are small but we are many*
> *We are many, we are small*
> *We were here before you rose*
> *We will be here when you fall.*

Their voices were high and whispery and slightly whiny. They made Coraline feel uncomfortable.

Then Coraline dreamed a few commercials, and after that she dreamed of nothing at all.

She passed Coraline the stone with a hole in it.

CHAPTER 2

The next day it had stopped raining, but a thick white fog had lowered over the house.

'I'm going for a walk,' said Coraline.

'Don't go too far,' said her mother. 'And dress up warmly.'

Coraline put on her blue coat with a hood, her red scarf and her yellow wellington boots.

She went out.

Miss Spink was walking her dogs. 'Hello, Caroline,' said Miss Spink. 'Rotten weather.'

'Yes,' said Coraline.

'I played Portia once,' said Miss Spink. 'Miss Forcible talks about her Ophelia, but it was my Portia they came to see. When we trod the boards.'

Miss Spink was bundled up in pullovers and cardigans, so she seemed more small and circular than ever. She looked like a large, fluffy egg. She wore thick glasses that made her eyes seem huge.

'They used to send flowers to my dressing room. They *did*,' she said.

'Who did?' asked Coraline.

Miss Spink looked around cautiously, looking first over one shoulder and then over the other, peering into the mist as though someone might be listening.

'*Men*,' she whispered. Then she tugged the dogs to heel and waddled off back towards the house.

Coraline continued her walk.

She was three quarters of the way around the house when she saw Miss Forcible, standing at the door to the flat she shared with Miss Spink.

'Have you seen Miss Spink, Caroline?'

Coraline told her that she had, and that Miss Spink was out walking the dogs.

'I do hope she doesn't get lost; it'll bring on her shingles if she does, you'll see,' said Miss Forcible. 'You'd have to be an explorer to find your way around in this fog.'

'I'm an explorer,' said Coraline.

'Of course you are, lovey,' said Miss Forcible. 'Don't get lost, now.'

Coraline continued walking through the garden in the grey mist. She always kept in sight of the house. After about ten minutes of walking she found herself back where she had started.

The hair over her eyes was limp and wet, and her face felt damp.

'Ahoy! Caroline!' called the crazy old man upstairs.

'Oh, hello,' said Coraline.

She could hardly see the old man through the mist.

He walked down the steps on the outside of the house that led up past Coraline's front door to the door of his flat. He walked down very slowly. Coraline waited at the bottom of the steps.

'The mice do not like the mist,' he told her. 'It makes their whiskers droop.'

'I don't like the mist much, either,' admitted Coraline.

The old man leaned down, so close that the bottom of his moustache tickled Coraline's ear. 'The mice have a message for you,' he whispered.

Coraline didn't know what to say.

'The message is this. *Don't go through the door.*' He paused. 'Does that mean anything to you?'

'No,' said Coraline.

The old man shrugged. 'They are funny, the mice. They get things wrong. They got your name wrong, you know. They kept saying Coraline. Not

Caroline. Not Caroline at all.'

He picked up a milk bottle from the bottom step, and started back up to his attic flat.

Coraline went indoors. Her mother was working in her study. Her mother's study smelt of flowers.

'What shall I do?' asked Coraline.

'When do you go back to school?' asked her mother.

'Next week,' said Coraline.

'Hmph,' said her mother. 'I suppose I shall have to get you new school clothes. Remind me, dear, or else I'll forget,' and she went back to typing things on the computer screen.

'What shall I *do*?' repeated Coraline.

'Draw something.' Her mother passed her a sheet of paper and a ballpoint pen.

Coraline tried drawing the mist. After ten minutes of drawing she still had a white sheet of paper with

M ST
I

written on it in one corner, in slightly wiggly letters. She grunted and passed it to her mother.

'Mm. Very modern, dear,' said Coraline's mother.

Coraline crept into the drawing room and tried to open the old door in the corner. It was locked once more. She supposed her mother must have locked it again. She shrugged.

Coraline went to see her father.

He had his back to the door as he typed. 'Go away,' he said cheerfully as she walked in.

'I'm bored,' she said.

'Learn how to tap-dance,' he suggested, without turning round.

Coraline shook her head. 'Why don't you play with me?' she asked.

'Busy,' he said. 'Working,' he added. He still hadn't turned around to look at her. 'Why don't you go and bother Miss Spink and Miss Forcible?'

Coraline put on her coat and pulled up her hood and went out of the house. She went down the steps. She rang the door of Miss Spink and Miss Forcible's flat. Coraline could hear a frenzied woofing as the Scottie dogs ran out into the hall. After a while Miss Spink opened the door.

'Oh, it's you, Caroline,' she said. 'Angus, Hamish, Bruce, down now, loveys. It's only Caroline. Come in, dear. Would you like a cup of tea?'

The flat smelt of furniture polish and dogs.

'Yes, please,' said Coraline. Miss Spink led her into a dusty little room, which she called the parlour. On the walls were black and white photographs of pretty women, and theatre programmes in frames. Miss Forcible was sitting in one of the armchairs, knitting hard.

Miss Spink poured Coraline a cup of tea in a little pink bone-china cup with a saucer, and gave her a dry Garibaldi biscuit to go with it.

Miss Forcible looked at Miss Spink, picked up her knitting, and took a deep breath. 'Anyway, April. As I was saying: you still have to admit, there's life in the old dog yet,' she said.

'Miriam, dear, neither of us is as young as we were.'

'Madame Arcati,' replied Miss Forcible. 'The nurse in *Romeo*. Lady Bracknell. Character parts. They can't retire you from the stage.'

'Now, Miriam, we ag*reed*,' said Miss Spink.

Coraline wondered if they'd forgotten she was there. They weren't making much sense; she decided they were having an argument as old and comfortable as an armchair, the kind of argument that no one ever really wins or loses, but which can go on for ever, if both parties are willing.

She sipped her tea.

'I'll read the leaves, if you want,' said Miss Spink to Coraline.

'Sorry?' said Coraline.

'The tea leaves, dear. I'll read your future.'

Coraline passed Miss Spink her cup. Miss Spink peered short-sightedly at the black tea leaves in the bottom. She pursed her lips.

'You know, Caroline,' she said after a while, 'you are in terrible danger.'

Miss Forcible snorted and put down her knitting. 'Don't be silly, April. Stop scaring the girl. Your eyes are going. Pass me that cup, child.'

Coraline carried the cup over to Miss Forcible. Miss Forcible looked into it carefully, and shook her head, and looked into it again.

'Oh dear,' she said. 'You were right, April. She *is* in danger.'

'See, Miriam,' said Miss Spink triumphantly. 'My eyes are as good as they ever were . . .'

'What am I in danger from?' asked Coraline.

Misses Spink and Forcible stared at her blankly. 'It didn't say,' said Miss Spink. 'Tea leaves aren't reliable for that kind of thing. Not really. They're good for generalities, but not for specifics.'

'What should I do then?' asked Coraline, who was slightly alarmed by this.

'Don't wear green in your dressing room,' suggested Miss Spink.

'Or mention the Scottish play,' added Miss Forcible.

Coraline wondered why so few of the adults she had met made any sense. She sometimes wondered who they thought they were talking to.

'And be very, very careful,' said Miss Spink. She got up from her armchair and went over to the fireplace. On the mantelpiece was a small jar, and Miss Spink took off the top of the jar and began to pull things out of it. There was a tiny china duck, a thimble, a strange little brass coin, two paperclips, and a stone with a hole in it.

She passed Coraline the stone with a hole in it.

'What's it for?' asked Coraline. The hole went all the way through the middle of the stone. She held it up to the window and looked through it.

'It might help,' said Miss Spink. 'They're good for bad things, sometimes.'

Coraline put on her coat, said goodbye to Misses Spink and Forcible, and to the dogs, and went outside.

The mist hung like blindness around the house. She walked slowly to the steps up to her family's flat, and then stopped and looked around.

In the mist, it was a ghost-world. *In danger?* thought Coraline to herself. It sounded exciting. It didn't sound like a bad thing. Not really.

Coraline went back up the steps, her fist closed tightly around her new stone.

Her eyes were big black buttons.

CHAPTER 3

The next day the sun shone, and Coraline's mother took her into the nearest large town to buy clothes for school. They dropped her father off at the railway station. He was going into London for the day to see some people.

Coraline waved him goodbye.

They went to the department store to buy the school clothes.

Coraline saw some Day-Glo green gloves she liked a lot. Her mother refused to get them for her, preferring instead to buy white socks, navy-blue school underpants, four grey blouses, and a dark grey skirt.

'But Mum, *everybody* at school's got grey blouses and everything. *Nobody's* got green gloves. I could be the only one.'

Her mother ignored her; she was talking to the

shop assistant. They were talking about which kind of pullover to get for Coraline, and were agreeing that the best thing to do would be to get one that was embarrassingly large and baggy, in the hope that one day she might grow into it.

Coraline wandered off, and looked at a display of wellington boots shaped like frogs and ducks and rabbits.

Then she wandered back.

'Coraline? Oh, there you are. Where on earth were you?'

'I was kidnapped by aliens,' said Coraline. 'They came down from outer space with ray guns, but I fooled them by wearing a wig and laughing in a foreign accent, and I escaped.'

'Yes, dear. Now, I think you could do with some more hairclips, don't you?'

'No.'

'Well, let's say half a dozen, to be on the safe side,' said her mother.

Coraline didn't say anything.

In the car on the way back home, Coraline said, 'What's in the empty flat?'

'I don't know. Nothing, I expect. It probably looks like our flat before we moved in. Empty rooms.'

'Do you think you could get into it from our flat?'

'Not unless you can walk through bricks, dear.'

'Oh.'

They got home around lunchtime. The sun was shining, although the day was cold. Coraline's mother looked in the fridge, and found a sad little tomato and a piece of cheese with green stuff growing on it. There was only a crust in the bread bin.

'I'd better dash down to the shops and get some fishfingers or something,' said her mother. 'Do you want to come?'

'No,' said Coraline.

'Suit yourself,' said her mother, and left. Then she came back and got her purse and car keys and went out again.

Coraline was bored.

She flipped through a book her mother was reading about native people in a distant country; how every day they would take pieces of white silk and draw on them in wax, then dip the silks in dye, then draw on them more in wax and dye them some more, then boil the wax out in hot water, and then, finally, throw the now-beautiful cloths on a fire and burn them to ashes.

It seemed particularly pointless to Coraline, but she hoped that the people enjoyed it.

She was still bored, and her mother wasn't yet home.

Coraline got a chair and pushed it over to the kitchen door. She climbed on to the chair, and reached up. She clambered down, and got a broom from the broom cupboard. She climbed back on the chair again, and reached up with the broom.

Chink.

She climbed down from the chair and picked up the keys. She smiled triumphantly. Then she leaned the broom against the wall and went into the drawing room.

The family did not use the drawing room. They had inherited the furniture from Coraline's grandmother, along with a wooden coffee table, a side table, a heavy glass ashtray and the oil painting of a bowl of fruit. Coraline could never work out why anyone would want to paint a bowl of fruit. Other than that, the room was empty: there were no knick-knacks on the mantelpiece, no statues or clocks; nothing that made it feel comfortable or lived-in.

The old black key felt colder than any of the others. She pushed it into the keyhole. It turned smoothly, with a satisfying clunk.

Coraline stopped and listened. She knew she was doing something wrong, and she was trying to listen for her mother coming back, but she heard nothing. Then Coraline put her hand on the doorknob and turned it; and, finally, she opened the door.

It opened on to a dark hallway. The bricks had gone, as if they'd never been there. There was a cold, musty smell coming through the open doorway: it smelled like something very old and very slow.

Coraline went through the door.

She wondered what the empty flat would be like – if that was where the corridor led.

Coraline walked down the corridor uneasily. There was something very familiar about it.

The carpet beneath her feet was the same carpet they had in their flat. The wallpaper was the same wallpaper they had. The picture hanging in the hall was the same that they had hanging in their hallway at home.

She knew where she was: she was in her own home. She hadn't left.

She shook her head, confused.

She stared at the picture hanging on the wall: no, it wasn't exactly the same. The picture they had in their own hallway showed a boy in old-fashioned clothes staring at some bubbles. But now the expression on his face was different – he was looking at the bubbles as if he was planning to do something very nasty indeed to them. And there was something peculiar about his eyes.

Coraline stared at his eyes, trying to work out what exactly was different.

She almost had it when somebody said, 'Coraline?'

It sounded like her mother. Coraline went into the kitchen, where the voice had come from. A woman stood in the kitchen with her back to Coraline. She looked a little like Coraline's mother. Only . . .

Only her skin was white as paper.

Only she was taller and thinner.

Only her fingers were too long, and they never stopped moving, and her dark-red fingernails were curved and sharp.

'Coraline?' the woman said. 'Is that you?'

And then she turned round. Her eyes were big black buttons.

'Lunchtime, Coraline,' said the woman.

'Who are you?' asked Coraline.

'I'm your other mother,' said the woman. 'Go and tell your other father that lunch is ready.' She opened the door of the oven. Suddenly Coraline realised how hungry she was. It smelled wonderful. 'Well, go on.'

Coraline went down the hall, to where her father's study was. She opened the door. There was a man in there, sitting at the keyboard, with his back to her. 'Hello,' said Coraline. 'I – I mean, she said to say that lunch is ready.'

The man turned round.

His eyes were buttons – big and black and shiny.

'Hello, Coraline,' he said. 'I'm starving.'

He got up and went with her into the kitchen. They sat at the kitchen table and Coraline's other mother brought them lunch. A huge, golden-brown roasted chicken, fried potatoes, tiny green peas. Coraline shovelled the food into her mouth. It tasted wonderful.

'We've been waiting for you for a long time,' said Coraline's other father.

'For me?'

'Yes,' said the other mother. 'It wasn't the same here without you. But we knew you'd arrive one day, and then we could be a proper family. Would you like some more chicken?'

It was the best chicken that Coraline had ever eaten. Her mother sometimes made chicken, but it was always out of packets, or frozen, and was very dry, and it never tasted of anything. When Coraline's father cooked chicken he bought real chicken, but he did strange things to it, like stewing it in wine, or stuffing it with prunes, or baking it in pastry, and Coraline would always refuse to touch it on principle.

She took some more chicken.

'I didn't know I had another mother,' said Coraline cautiously.

'Of course you do. Everyone does,' said the other mother, her black-button eyes gleaming. 'After lunch I thought you might like to play in your room with the rats.'

'The rats?'

'From upstairs.'

Coraline had never seen a rat, except on television. She was quite looking forward to it. This was turning out to be a very interesting day after all.

After lunch her other parents did the washing-up, and Coraline went down the hall to her other bedroom.

It was different from her bedroom at home. For a start it was painted in an off-putting shade of green and a peculiar shade of pink.

Coraline decided that she wouldn't want to have to sleep in there; but that the colour scheme was an awful lot more interesting than the one in her own bedroom.

There were all sorts of remarkable things in there she'd never seen before: wind-up angels that fluttered around the bedroom like startled sparrows; books with pictures that writhed and crawled and shimmered; little dinosaur skulls that chattered their teeth as she passed. A whole toybox filled with wonderful toys.

This is more like it, thought Coraline. She looked out of the window. Outside, the view was the same one she saw from her own bedroom: trees, fields and, beyond them, on the horizon, distant purple hills.

Something black scurried across the floor and vanished under the bed. Coraline got down on her knees and looked under the bed. Fifty little red eyes stared back at her.

'Hello,' said Coraline. 'Are you the rats?'

They came out from under the bed, blinking their eyes in the light. They had short, soot-black fur, little red eyes, pink paws like tiny hands, and pink, hairless tails like long, smooth worms.

'Can you talk?' she asked.

The largest, blackest of the rats shook its head. It had an unpleasant sort of smile, Coraline thought.

'Well,' asked Coraline, 'what *do* you do?'

The rats formed a circle.

Then they began to climb on top of each other, carefully but swiftly, until they had formed a pyramid with the largest rat at the top.

The rats began to sing, in high, whispery voices,

We have teeth and we have tails
We have tails, we have eyes
We were here before you fell
You will be here when we rise.

It wasn't a pretty song. Coraline was sure she'd heard it before, or something like it, although she was unable to remember exactly where.

Then the pyramid fell apart, and the rats scampered, fast and black, towards the door.

The other crazy old man upstairs was standing in the doorway, holding a tall black hat in his hands. The rats scampered up him, burrowing into his pockets, into his shirt, up his trouser-legs, down his neck.

The largest rat climbed on to the old man's shoulders, swung up on the long grey moustache, past the big black-button eyes, and on to the top of the man's head.

In seconds the only evidence that the rats were there at all were the restless lumps under the man's clothes, forever sliding from place to place across him; and there was still the largest rat, who stared down, with glittering red eyes, at Coraline from the man's head.

The old man put his hat on, and the last rat was gone.

'Hello, Coraline,' said the other old man upstairs. 'I heard you were here. It is time for the rats to have their dinner. But you can come up with me, if you like, and watch them feed.'

There was something hungry in the old man's button eyes that made Coraline feel uncomfortable. 'No, thank you,' she said. 'I'm going outside to explore.'

The old man nodded, very slowly. Coraline could hear the rats whispering to each other, although she couldn't tell what they were saying.

She was not certain that she wanted to know what they were saying.

Her other parents stood in the kitchen doorway as she walked down the corridor, smiling identical smiles, and waving slowly. 'Have a nice time outside,' said her other mother.

'We'll just wait here for you to come back,' said her other father.

When Coraline got to the front door, she turned back and looked at them. They were still watching her, and waving, and smiling.

Coraline walked outside, and down the steps.

Miss Spink and Miss Forcible came on to the stage.

CHAPTER 4

The house looked exactly the same from the outside. Or almost exactly the same; around Miss Spink and Miss Forcible's door were blue and red light bulbs that flashed on and off spelling out words, the lights chasing each other around the door. On and off, around and around. ASTOUNDING! was followed by A THEATRICAL and then TRIUMPH!!!

It was a sunny, cold day, exactly like the one she'd left.

There was a polite noise from behind her.

She turned round. Standing on the wall next to her was a large black cat, identical to the large black cat she'd seen in the grounds at home.

'Good afternoon,' said the cat.

Its voice sounded like the voice at the back of Coraline's head, the voice she thought words in, but a man's voice, not a girl's.

'Hello,' said Coraline. 'I saw a cat like you in the garden at home. You must be the other cat.'

The cat shook its head. 'No,' it said. 'I'm not the other anything. I'm me.' It tipped its head on one side; green eyes glinted. 'You people are spread all over the place. Cats, on the other hand, keep ourselves together. If you see what I mean.'

'I suppose. But if you're the same cat I saw at home, how can you talk?'

Cats don't have shoulders, not like people do. But the cat shrugged, in one smooth movement that started at the tip of its tail and ended in a raised movement of its whiskers. 'I can talk.'

'Cats don't talk at home.'

'No?' said the cat.

'No,' said Coraline.

The cat leapt smoothly from the wall to the grass, near Coraline's feet. It stared up at her.

'Well, you're the expert on these things,' said the cat drily. 'After all, what would I know? I'm only a cat.'

It began to walk away, head and tail held high and proud.

'Come back,' said Coraline. 'Please. I'm sorry. I really am.'

The cat stopped walking, and sat down, and began to wash itself, thoughtfully, apparently unaware of Coraline's existence.

'We . . . we could be friends, you know,' said Coraline.

'We *could* be rare specimens of an exotic breed of African dancing elephants,' said the cat. 'But we're not. At least,' it added cattily, after darting a brief look at Coraline, 'I'*m* not.'

Coraline sighed.

'Please. What's your name?' Coraline asked the cat. 'Look, I'm Coraline. OK?'

The cat yawned slowly, carefully, revealing a mouth and tongue of astounding pinkness. 'Cats don't have names,' it said.

'No?' said Coraline.

'No,' said the cat. 'Now, *you* people have names. That's because you don't know who you are. We know who we are, so we don't need names.'

There was something irritatingly self-centred about the cat, Coraline decided. As if it were, in its opinion, the only thing in any world or place that could possibly be of any importance.

Half of her wanted to be very rude to it; the other half of her wanted to be polite and deferential. The polite half won.

'Please, what is this place?'

The cat glanced around briefly. 'It's here,' said the cat.

'I can see that. Well, how did you get here?'

'Like you did. I walked,' said the cat. 'Like this.'

Coraline watched as the cat walked slowly across the lawn. It walked behind a tree, but didn't come out the other side. Coraline went over to the tree and looked behind it. The cat was gone.

She walked back towards the house. There was another polite noise from behind her. It was the cat.

'By the by,' it said. 'It was sensible of you to bring protection. I'd hang on to it, if I were you.'

'Protection?'

'That's what I said,' said the cat. 'And anyway –'

It paused, and stared intently at something that wasn't there.

Then it went down into a low crouch and moved slowly forward, two or three steps. It seemed to be stalking an invisible mouse. Abruptly, it turned tail and dashed for the woods.

It vanished among the trees.

Coraline wondered what the cat had meant.

She also wondered whether cats could all talk where she came from and just chose not to, or whether they could only talk when they were here – wherever *here* was.

She walked down the brick steps to the Misses Spink and Forcible's front door. The blue and red lights flashed on and off.

The door was open, just slightly. She knocked on it, but her first knock made the door swing open, and Coraline went in.

She was in a dark room that smelled of dust and velvet. The door swung shut behind her, and the room was black. Coraline edged forward into a small anteroom. Her face brushed against something soft. It was cloth. She reached up her hand and pushed at the cloth. It parted.

She stood blinking on the other side of the velvet curtains, in a poorly lit theatre. Far away, at the edge of the room, was a high wooden stage, empty and bare, a dim spotlight shining on to it from above.

There were seats between Coraline and the stage. Rows and rows of seats. She heard a shuffling noise, and a light came towards her, swinging from side to side. When it was closer she saw the light was coming from a torch being carried in the mouth of a large black Scottie dog, its muzzle grey with age.

'Hello,' said Coraline.

The dog put the torch down on the floor and looked up at her. 'Right. Let's see your ticket,' it said gruffly.

'Ticket?'

'That's what I said. Ticket. I haven't got all day,

you know. You can't watch the show without a ticket.'

Coraline sighed. 'I don't have a ticket,' she admitted.

'Another one,' said the dog gloomily. 'Come in here, bold as anything, "Where's your ticket?" "Haven't got one." I don't know . . .' It shook its head, then shrugged. 'Come on, then.'

The dog picked up the torch in its mouth and trotted off into the dark. Coraline followed. When it got near to the front of the stage it stopped and shone the torch on to an empty seat. Coraline sat down and the dog wandered off.

As her eyes got used to the darkness she realised that the other inhabitants of the seats were also dogs.

There was a sudden hissing noise from behind the stage. Coraline decided it was the sound of a scratchy old record being put on to a record player. The hissing became the noise of trumpets, and Miss Spink and Miss Forcible came on to the stage.

Miss Spink was riding a one-wheeled bicycle, and juggling balls. Miss Forcible skipped on behind her, holding a basket of flowers. She scattered the flower petals across the stage as she went. They reached the front of the stage, and Miss Spink leapt nimbly off the unicycle, and the two old women bowed low.

All the dogs thumped their tails and barked enthusiastically. Coraline clapped politely.

Then they unbuttoned their fluffy round coats and opened them. But their coats weren't all that opened: their faces opened, too, like empty shells, and out of the old empty fluffy round bodies stepped two young women. They were thin, and pale, and quite pretty, and had black-button eyes.

The new Miss Spink was wearing green tights and high brown boots that went most of the way up her legs. The new Miss Forcible wore a white dress and had flowers in her long yellow hair.

Coraline pressed back against her seat.

Miss Spink left the stage, and the noise of trumpets squealed as the gramophone needle dug its way across the record and was pulled off.

'This is my favourite bit,' whispered the little dog in the seat next to her.

The other Miss Forcible picked a knife out of a box on the corner of the stage. 'Is this a dagger that I see before me?' she asked.

'Yes!' shouted all the little dogs. 'It is!' Miss Forcible curtseyed, and all the dogs applauded again. Coraline didn't bother clapping this time.

Miss Spink came back on. She slapped her thigh, and all the little dogs woofed.

'And now,' Miss Spink said, 'Miriam and I proudly present a new and exciting addendum to our theatrical exposition. Do I see a volunteer?'

The little dog next to Coraline nudged her with its front paw. 'That's you,' it hissed.

Coraline stood up, and walked up the wooden steps to the stage.

'Can I have a big round of applause for the young volunteer?' asked Miss Spink. The dogs woofed and squealed and thumped their tails on the velvet seats.

'Now, Coraline,' said Miss Spink. 'What's your name?'

'Coraline,' said Coraline.

'And we don't know each other, do we?'

Coraline looked at the thin young woman with black-button eyes and shook her head, slowly.

'Now,' said the other Miss Spink, 'stand over here.' She led Coraline over to a board by the side of the stage, and put a balloon on top of Coraline's head.

Miss Spink walked over to Miss Forcible. She blindfolded Miss Forcible's button eyes with a black scarf and put the knife into her hands. Then she turned her round three or four times and pointed her at Coraline. Coraline held her breath and squeezed her fingers into two tight fists.

Miss Forcible threw the knife at the balloon. It popped loudly, and the knife stuck into the board just above Coraline's head and twanged there. Coraline breathed out.

The dogs went wild.

Miss Spink gave Coraline a very small box of chocolates and thanked her for being such a good sport. Coraline went back to her seat.

'You were very good,' said the little dog.

'Thank you,' said Coraline.

Misses Forcible and Spink began juggling with huge wooden clubs. Coraline opened the box of chocolates. The little dog looked at them longingly.

'Would you like one?' she asked it.

'Yes, please,' whispered the dog. 'Only not toffee ones. They make me drool.'

'I thought chocolates weren't very good for dogs,' she said, remembering something Miss Forcible had once told her.

'Maybe where you come from,' whispered the little dog. 'Here, it's all we eat.'

Coraline couldn't see what the chocolates were, in the dark. She took an experimental bite of one which turned out to be coconut. Coraline didn't like coconut. She gave it to the dog.

'Thank you,' said the dog.

'You're welcome,' said Coraline.

Miss Forcible and Miss Spink were doing some acting. Miss Forcible was sitting on a stepladder, and Miss Spink was standing at the bottom.

'What's in a name?' asked Miss Forcible. 'That which we call a rose by any other name would smell as sweet.'

'Have you got any more chocolates?' said the dog.

Coraline gave the dog another chocolate.

'I know not how to tell thee who I am,' said Miss Spink to Miss Forcible.

'This bit finishes soon,' whispered the dog. 'Then they start folk dancing.'

'How long does this go on for?' asked Coraline. 'The theatre?'

'All the time,' said the dog. 'For ever and always.'

'Here,' said Coraline. 'Keep the chocolates.'

'Thank you,' said the dog. Coraline stood up.

'See you soon,' said the dog.

'Bye,' said Coraline. She walked out of the theatre and back into the garden. She had to blink her eyes at the daylight.

Her other parents were waiting for her in the garden, standing side by side. They were smiling.

'Did you have a nice time?' asked her other mother.

'It was interesting,' said Coraline.

The three of them walked back up to Coraline's other house together. Coraline's other mother stroked Coraline's hair with her long white fingers. Coraline shook her head.

'Don't do that,' said Coraline.

Her other mother took her hand away.

'So,' said her other father. 'Do you like it here?'

'I suppose,' said Coraline. 'It's much more interesting than at home.'

They went inside.

'I'm glad you like it,' said Coraline's other mother. 'Because we'd like to think that this is your home. You can stay here for ever and always. If you want to.'

'Hmm,' said Coraline. She put her hands in her pockets and thought about it. Her fingertips touched the stone that the real Misses Spink and Forcible had given her the day before, the stone with the hole in it.

'If you want to stay,' said her other father. 'There's only one little thing we'll have to do, so you can stay here for ever and always.'

They went into the kitchen. On a china plate on the kitchen table were a spool of black cotton and a long silver needle and, beside them, two large black buttons.

'I don't think so,' said Coraline.

'Oh, but we want you to,' said her other mother. 'We want you to stay. And it's just a little thing.'

'It won't hurt,' said her other father.

Coraline knew that when grown-ups told you something wouldn't hurt it almost always did. She shook her head.

Her other mother smiled brightly and the hair on her head drifted like plants under the sea. 'We only want what's best for you,' she said.

She put her hand on Coraline's shoulder. Coraline backed away.

'I'm going now,' said Coraline. She put her hands back in her pockets. Her fingers closed around the stone with the hole in.

Her other mother's hand scuttled off Coraline's shoulder like a frightened spider.

'If that's what you want,' she said.

'Yes,' said Coraline.

'We'll see you soon, though,' said her other father. 'When you come back.'

'Um,' said Coraline.

'And then we'll all be together as one big happy family,' said her other mother. 'For ever and always.'

Coraline backed away. She turned and hurried into the drawing room and pulled open the door in the corner. There was no brick wall there now – just darkness; a night-black underground darkness that seemed as if things in it might be moving.

Coraline hesitated. She turned back. Her other mother and her other father were walking towards her, holding hands. They were looking at her with their black-button eyes. Or at least she *thought* they were looking at her. She couldn't be sure.

Her other mother reached out her free hand and beckoned gently with one white finger. Her pale lips mouthed, 'Come back soon,' although she said nothing aloud.

Coraline took a deep breath and stepped into the darkness, where strange voices whispered and distant winds howled. She became certain that there was something in the dark behind her: something very old and very slow. Her heart beat so hard and so loudly she was scared it would burst out of her chest. She closed her eyes against the dark.

Eventually she bumped into something, and opened her eyes, startled. She had bumped into an armchair, in her drawing room.

The open doorway behind her was blocked by rough red bricks.

She was home.

'You will always be safe here with me.'

CHAPTER 5

Coraline locked the door of the drawing room with the cold black key.

She went back into the kitchen, and climbed on to a chair. She tried to put the bunch of keys back on top of the door again. She tried four or five times before she was forced to accept that she just wasn't big enough, and she put them down on the counter next to the door.

Her mother still hadn't returned from her shopping expedition.

Coraline went to the freezer and took out the spare loaf of frozen bread in the bottom compartment. She made herself some toast, with jam and peanut butter. She drank a glass of water.

She waited for her parents to come back.

When it began to get dark, Coraline microwaved herself a frozen pizza.

Then Coraline watched television. She wondered why grown-ups gave themselves all the good programmes, with all the shouting and running around in.

After a while she started yawning. Then she undressed, brushed her teeth and put herself to bed.

In the morning she went into her parents' room, but their bed hadn't been slept in, and they weren't around. She ate tinned spaghetti for breakfast.

For lunch she had a block of cooking chocolate and an apple. The apple was yellow and slightly shrivelled, but it tasted sweet and good.

For tea she went down to see Misses Spink and Forcible. She had three digestive biscuits, a glass of limeade, and a cup of weak tea. The limeade was very interesting. It didn't taste anything like limes. It tasted bright green and vaguely chemical. Coraline liked it enormously. She wished they had it at home.

'How are your dear mother and father?' asked Miss Spink.

'Missing,' said Coraline. 'I haven't seen either of them since yesterday. I'm on my own. I think I've probably become a single child family.'

'Tell your mother that we found the Glasgow Empire press clippings we were telling her about.

She seemed very interested when Miriam mentioned them to her.'

'She's vanished under mysterious circumstances,' said Coraline, 'and I believe my father has as well.'

'I'm afraid we'll be out all day tomorrow, Caroline lovey,' said Miss Forcible. 'We'll be staying with April's niece in Royal Tunbridge Wells.'

They showed Coraline a photographic album, with photographs of Miss Spink's niece in it, and then Coraline went home.

She opened her money box and walked down to the supermarket. She bought two large bottles of limeade, a chocolate cake, and a new bag of apples, and went back home and ate them for dinner.

She cleaned her teeth, and went into her father's office. She woke up his computer and wrote a story.

CORALINE'S STORY

THERE WAS A GIRL HER NAME WAS APPLE. SHE USED TO DANCE A LOT. SHE DANCED AND DANCED UNTIL HER FEET TURND INTO SOSSAJES. THE END.

She printed out the story and turned off the computer. Then she drew a picture of the little girl dancing underneath the words on the paper.

She ran herself a bath with too much bubble bath in it, and the bubbles ran over the side and went all over the floor. She dried herself, and the floor as best she could, and went to bed.

Coraline woke up in the night. She went into her parents' bedroom, but the bed was made and empty. The glowing green numbers on the digital clock glowed 3:12 a.m.

All alone, in the middle of the night, Coraline began to cry. There was no other sound in the empty flat.

She climbed into her parents' bed, and, after a while, she went back to sleep.

Coraline was woken by cold paws batting her face. She opened her eyes. Big green eyes stared back at her. It was the cat.

'Hello,' said Coraline. 'How did you get in?'

The cat didn't say anything. Coraline got out of bed. She was wearing a long T-shirt and pyjama bottoms. 'Have you come to tell me something?'

The cat yawned, which made its eyes flash green.

'Do you know where Mummy and Daddy are?'

The cat blinked at her slowly.

'Is that a yes?'

The cat blinked again. Coraline decided that that was indeed a yes. 'Will you take me to them?'

The cat stared at her. Then it walked out into the hall. She followed. It walked the length of the corridor and stopped down at the very end, where a full-length mirror hung. The mirror had been, a long time before, the inside of a wardrobe door. It had been hanging there on the wall when they moved in, and, although Coraline's mother had spoken occasionally of replacing it with something newer, she never had.

Coraline turned on the light in the hall.

The mirror showed the corridor behind her; that was only to be expected. But also reflected in the mirror were her parents. They stood awkwardly in the reflection of the hall. They seemed sad and alone. As Coraline watched, they waved to her, slowly, with limp hands. Coraline's father had his arm around her mother.

In the mirror Coraline's mother and father stared at her. Her father opened his mouth and said something, but she could hear nothing at all. Her mother breathed on the inside of the mirror-glass, and quickly, before the fog faded, she wrote:

HELP US

with the tip of her forefinger. The fog on the inside of the mirror faded, and so did her parents, and now the mirror reflected only the corridor, and Coraline, and the cat.

'Where are they?' Coraline asked the cat. The cat made no reply, but Coraline could imagine its voice, dry as a dead fly on a windowsill in winter, saying, *Well, where do you think they are?*

'They aren't going to come back, are they?' said Coraline. 'Not under their own steam.'

The cat blinked at her. Coraline took it as a yes.

'Right,' said Coraline. 'Then I suppose there is only one thing left to do.'

She walked into her father's study. She sat down at his desk. Then she picked up the telephone, and opened the phone book and called the local police station.

'Police,' said a gruff male voice.

'Hello,' she said. 'My name is Coraline Jones.'

'You're up a bit after your bedtime, aren't you, young lady?' said the policeman.

'Possibly,' said Coraline, who was not going to be diverted, 'but I am ringing to report a crime.'

'And what sort of crime would that be?'

'Kidnapping. Grown-up-napping, really. My parents have been stolen away into a world on the other side of the mirror in our hall.'

'And do you know who stole them?' asked the police officer. Coraline could hear the smile in his voice, and she tried extra hard to sound like an adult might sound, to make him take her seriously.

'I think my other mother has them both in her clutches. She may want to keep them and sew their eyes with black buttons, or she may simply have them in order to lure me back into reach of her fingers. I'm not sure.'

'Ah. The nefarious clutches of her fiendish fingers, is it?' he said. 'Mm. You know what I suggest, Miss Jones?'

'No,' said Coraline. 'What?'

'You ask your mother to make you a big old mug of hot chocolate, and then give you a great big old hug. There's nothing like hot chocolate and a hug for making the nightmares go away. And if she starts to tell you off for waking her up at this time of night, why, you tell her that that's what the policeman said.' He had a deep, reassuring voice.

Coraline was not reassured.

'When I see her,' said Coraline, 'I shall tell her that.' And she put down the telephone.

The black cat, who had sat on the floor grooming its fur through this entire conversation, now stood up and led the way into the hall.

Coraline went back into her bedroom and put on her blue dressing gown and her slippers. She looked under the sink for a torch, and found one, but the batteries had long since run down and it barely glowed with the faintest straw-coloured light. She put it down again and found a box of in-case-of-emergency white wax candles, and thrust one into a candlestick. She put an apple into each pocket. She picked up the ring of keys and took the old black key off the ring.

She walked into the drawing room and looked at the door. She had the feeling that the door was looking back at her, which she knew was silly, and knew on a deeper level was somehow true.

She went back into her bedroom, and rummaged in the pocket of her jeans. She found the stone with the hole in it, and put it into her dressing-gown pocket.

She lit the candle wick with a match and watched it sputter and light, then she picked up the black key. It was cold in her hand. She put the key into the keyhole in the door, but did not turn it.

'When I was a little girl,' said Coraline to the cat, 'when we lived in our old house, a long, long time ago, my dad took me for a walk on the waste-land between our house and the shops.

'It wasn't the best place to go for a walk, really. There were all these things that people had thrown away back there – old cookers and broken dishes and dolls with no arms and no legs, and empty cans and broken bottles. Mum and Dad made me promise not to go exploring back there, because there were too many sharp things, and tetanus and such.

'But I kept telling them I wanted to explore it. So one day my dad put on his big brown boots and his gloves and put my boots on me and my jeans and sweater, and we went for a walk.

'We must have walked for about twenty minutes. We went down this hill, to the bottom of a gully, where a stream was, when my dad suddenly said to me, "Coraline – run away. Up the hill. Now!" He said it in a tight sort of way, urgently, so I did. I ran away up the hill. Something hurt me on the back of my arm as I ran, but I kept running.

'As I got to the top of the hill I heard somebody thundering up the hill behind me. It was my dad, charging like a rhino. When he reached me he picked me up in his arms and swept me over the edge of the hill.

'And then we stopped and we puffed and we panted, and we looked back down the gully.

'The air was alive with yellow wasps. We must have stepped on a wasps' nest in a rotten branch as we walked. And while I was running up the hill, my dad stayed and got stung, to give me time to run away. His glasses had fallen off when he ran.

'I only had the one sting on the back of my arm. He had thirty-nine stings, all over him. We counted later, in the bath.'

The black cat began to wash its face and whiskers in a manner that indicated increasing impatience. Coraline reached down and stroked the back of its head and neck. The cat stood up, walked several paces until it was out of her reach, then it sat down and looked up at her again.

'So,' said Coraline, 'later that afternoon my dad went back again to the wasteland, to get his glasses back. He said if he left it another day he wouldn't be able to remember where they'd fallen.

'And soon he got home, wearing his glasses. He said that he wasn't scared when he was standing there and the wasps were stinging him and hurting him and he was watching me run away. Because he knew he had to give me enough time to run, or the wasps would have come after both of us.'

Coraline turned the key in the door. It turned with a loud clunk.

The door swung open.

There was no brick wall on the other side of the door: only darkness. A cold wind blew through the passageway.

Coraline made no move to walk through the door.

'And he said that wasn't brave of him, doing that, just standing there and being stung,' said Coraline to the cat. 'It wasn't brave because he wasn't scared: it was the only thing he could do. But going back again to get his glasses, when he knew the wasps were there, when he was really scared. That was brave.'

She took her first step down the dark corridor.

She could smell dust and damp and mustiness.

The cat padded along beside her.

'And why was that?' asked the cat, although it sounded barely interested.

'Because,' she said, 'when you're scared but you still do it anyway, that's brave.'

The candle cast huge, strange, flickering shadows along the wall. She heard something moving in the darkness, beside her, or to one side of her, she could not tell. It seemed as if it was keeping pace with her, whatever it was.

'And that's why you're going back to her world, then?' said the cat. 'Because your father once saved you from wasps?'

'Don't be silly,' said Coraline. 'I'm going back for them because they are my parents. And if they noticed I was gone I'm sure they would do the same for me. You know you're talking again?'

'How fortunate I am,' said the cat, 'in having a

travelling companion of such wisdom and intelligence.' Its tone remained sarcastic, but its fur was bristling, and its brush of a tail stuck up in the air.

Coraline was going to say something, like *sorry* or *wasn't it a lot shorter walk last time?* when the candle went out as suddenly as if it had been snuffed by someone's hand.

There was a scrabbling and a pattering, and Coraline could feel her heart pounding against her ribs. She put out one hand . . . and felt something wispy, like a spider's web, brush her hands and her face.

At the end of the corridor the electric light went on, blinding after the darkness. A woman stood, silhouetted by the light, a little ahead of Coraline.

'Coraline? Darling?' she called.

'Mum!' said Coraline, and she ran forward, eager and relieved.

'Darling,' said the woman. 'Why did you ever run away from me?'

Coraline was too close to stop, and she felt the other mother's cold arms enfold her. She stood there, rigid and trembling as the other mother held her tightly.

'Where are my parents?' Coraline asked.

'We're here,' said her other mother, in a voice

so close to her real mother's that Coraline could scarcely tell them apart. 'We're here. We're ready to love you and play with you and feed you and make your life interesting.'

Coraline pulled back, and the other mother let her go, with reluctance.

The other father, who had been sitting on a chair in the hallway, stood up and smiled. 'Come on into the kitchen,' he said. 'I'll make us a midnight snack. And you'll want something to drink – hot chocolate, perhaps?'

Coraline walked down the hallway until she reached the mirror at the end. There was nothing reflected in it but a young girl in her dressing gown and slippers, who looked like she had recently been crying but whose eyes were real eyes, not black buttons, and who was holding tightly to a burned-out candle in a candlestick.

She looked at the girl in the mirror and the girl in the mirror looked back at her.

I *will be brave*, thought Coraline. No, I am *brave*.

She put down the candlestick on the floor, then she turned round. The other mother and the other father were looking at her hungrily.

'I don't need a snack,' she said. 'I have an apple. See?' And she took an apple from her dressing-gown pocket, then bit into it with relish and an enthusiasm that she did not really feel.

The other father looked disappointed. The other mother smiled, showing a full set of teeth, and each of the teeth was a tiny bit too long. The lights in the hallway made her black-button eyes glitter and gleam.

'You don't frighten me,' said Coraline, although they did frighten her, very much. 'I want my parents back.'

The world seemed to shimmer a little at the edges.

'Whatever would I have done with your old parents? If they have left you, Coraline, it must be because they became bored with you, or tired. Now, I will never become bored with you, and I will never abandon you. You will always be safe here with me.' The other mother's wet-looking black hair drifted around her head, like the tentacles of a creature in the deep ocean.

'They weren't bored of me,' said Coraline. 'You're lying. You stole them.'

'Silly, silly Coraline. They are fine wherever they are.'

Coraline simply glared at the other mother.

'I'll prove it,' said the other mother, and brushed the surface of the mirror with her long white fingers. It clouded over, as if a dragon had breathed on it, and then it cleared.

In the mirror it was daytime already. Coraline was looking at the hallway, all the way down to her front door. The door opened from the outside and Coraline's mother and father walked inside. They carried suitcases.

'That was a fine holiday,' said Coraline's father.

'How nice it is, not to have Coraline any more,' said her mother with a happy smile. 'Now we can do all the things we always wanted to do, like go abroad, but were prevented from doing by having a little daughter.'

'And,' said her father, 'I take great comfort in knowing that her other mother will take better care of her than we ever could.'

The mirror fogged and faded and reflected the night once more.

'See?' said her other mother.

'No,' said Coraline. 'I don't see. And I don't believe it either.'

She hoped that what she had just seen was not real, but she was not as certain as she sounded. There was a tiny doubt inside her, like a maggot in an apple core. Then she looked up and saw the expression on her other mother's face: a flash of real anger, which crossed her face like summer lightning, and Coraline was sure in her heart that what she had seen in the mirror was no more than an illusion.

Coraline sat down on the sofa and ate her apple.

'Please,' said her other mother. 'Don't be difficult.' She walked into the drawing room and clapped her hands twice. There was a rustling noise and a black rat appeared. It stared up at her. 'Bring me the key,' she said.

The rat chittered, then it ran through the open door that led back to Coraline's own flat.

The rat returned, dragging the key behind it.

'Why don't you have your own key on this side?' asked Coraline.

'There is only one key. Only one door,' said the other father.

'Hush,' said the other mother. 'You must not bother our darling Coraline's head with such trivialities.' She put the key in the keyhole and twisted. The lock was stiff, but it clunked closed.

She dropped the key into her apron pocket.

Outside, the sky had begun to lighten to a luminous grey.

'If we aren't going to have a midnight snack,' said the other mother, 'we still need our beauty sleep. I am going back to bed, Coraline. I would strongly suggest that you do the same.'

She placed her long white fingers on the

shoulders of the other father, and she walked him out of the room.

Coraline walked over to the door at the far corner of the drawing room. She tugged on it, but it was tightly locked. The door of her other parents' bedroom was now closed.

She was indeed tired, but she did not want to sleep in the bedroom. She did not want to sleep under the same roof as her other mother.

The front door was not locked. Coraline walked out into the dawn and down the stone steps. She sat down on the bottom step. It was cold.

Something furry pushed itself against her side in one smooth, insinuating motion. Coraline jumped, then breathed a sigh of relief when she saw what it was.

'Oh. It's you,' she said to the black cat.

'See?' said the cat. 'It wasn't so hard recognising me, was it? Even without names.'

'Well, what if I wanted to call you?'

The cat wrinkled its nose and managed to look unimpressed. 'Calling cats,' it confided, 'tends to be a rather overrated activity. Might as well call a whirlwind.'

'What if it was dinnertime?' asked Coraline. 'Wouldn't you want to be called then?'

'Of course,' said the cat. 'But a simple cry of

'Dinner!' would do nicely. See? No need for names.'

'Why does she want me?' Coraline asked the cat. 'Why does she want me to stay here with her?'

'She wants something to love, I think,' said the cat. 'Something that isn't her. She might want something to eat as well. It's hard to tell with creatures like that.'

'Do you have any advice?' asked Coraline.

The cat looked as if it were about to say something else sarcastic. Then it flicked its whiskers, and said, 'Challenge her. There's no guarantee she'll play fair, but her kind of thing loves games and challenges.'

'What kind of thing is that?' asked Coraline.

But the cat made no answer, simply stretched, luxuriantly, and walked away. Then it stopped, and turned, and said, 'I'd go inside if I were you. Get some sleep. You have a long day ahead of you.'

And then the cat was gone. Still, Coraline realised, it had a point. She crept back into the silent house, past the closed bedroom door beyond which the other mother and the other father . . . what? she wondered. Slept? Waited? And then it came to her that, should she open the bedroom door, she would find it empty, or, more precisely, that it was an empty room and it would remain

76

empty until the exact moment that she opened the door.

Somehow, that made it easier. Coraline walked into the green and pink parody of her own bedroom. She closed the door and hauled the toybox in front of it – it would not keep anyone out, but the noise somebody would make trying to dislodge it would wake her, she hoped.

The toys in the toybox were still mostly asleep, and they stirred and muttered as she moved their box, and then they went back to sleep. Coraline checked under her bed, looking for rats, but there was nothing there. She took off her dressing gown and slippers and climbed into bed and fell asleep with barely enough time to reflect, as she did so, on what the cat could have meant by *a challenge*.

There was no ground beneath her feet, just
a misty, milky whiteness.

CHAPTER 6

Coraline was woken by the mid-morning sun, full on her face.

For a moment she felt utterly dislocated. She did not know where she was; she was not entirely sure *who* she was. It is astonishing just how much of what we are can be tied to the beds we wake up in in the morning, and it is astonishing how fragile that can be.

Sometimes Coraline would forget who she was while she was daydreaming that she was exploring the Arctic, or the Amazon rainforest, or darkest Africa, and it was not until someone tapped her on the shoulder or said her name that Coraline would come back from a million miles away with a start, and all in a fraction of a second have to remember who she was, and what her name was, and that she was even there at all.

Now there was sun on her face, and she was Coraline Jones. Yes. And then the green and pinkness of the room she was in, and the rustling of a large painted paper butterfly as it fluttered and beat its way about the ceiling, told her where she had woken up.

She climbed out of the bed. She could not wear her pyjamas, dressing gown and slippers during the day, she decided, even if it meant wearing the other Coraline's clothes. (Was there an other Coraline? No, she decided, there wasn't. There was just her.) There were no proper clothes in the cupboard, though. They were more like dressing-up clothes or (she thought) the kind of clothes she would love to have hanging in her own wardrobe at home: there was a raggedy witch costume; a patched scarecrow costume; a future-warrior costume with little digital lights on it that glittered and blinked; a slinky evening dress all covered in feathers and mirrors. Finally, in a drawer, she found a pair of black jeans that seemed to be made of velvet night, and a grey sweater the colour of thick smoke with faint and tiny stars in the fabric which twinkled.

She pulled on the jeans and the sweater. Then she put on a pair of bright-orange boots she found at the bottom of the cupboard.

She took her last apple out of the pocket of her

dressing gown, and then, from the same pocket, the stone with the hole in it.

She put the stone into the pocket of her jeans, and it was as if her head had cleared a little. As if she had come out of some sort of a fog.

She went into the kitchen, but it was deserted.

Still, she was sure that there was someone in the flat. She walked down the hall until she reached her father's study, and discovered that it was occupied.

'Where's the other mother?' she asked the other father. He was sitting in the study, at a desk which looked just like her father's, but he was not doing anything at all, not even reading gardening catalogues as her own father did when he was only pretending to be working.

'Out,' he told her. 'Fixing the doors. There are some vermin problems.' He seemed pleased to have somebody to talk to.

'The rats, you mean?'

'No, the rats are our friends. This is the other kind, big black fellow, with his tail high.'

'The cat, you mean?'

'That's the one,' said her other father.

He looked less like her true father today. There was something slightly vague about his face – like bread dough that had begun to rise, smoothing out the bumps and cracks and depressions.

'Really, I mustn't talk to you when she's not here,' he said. 'But don't you worry. She won't be gone often. I shall demonstrate our tender hospitality to you, such that you will not even think about ever going back.' He closed his mouth and folded his hands in his lap.

'So what am I to do now?' asked Coraline.

The other father pointed to his lips. *Silence.*

'If you won't even talk to me,' said Coraline, 'I am going exploring.'

'No point,' said the other father. 'There isn't anywhere but here. This is all she made: the house, the grounds, and the people in the house. She made it and she waited.' Then he looked embarrassed and he put one finger to his lips again, as if he had just said too much.

Coraline walked out of his study. She went into the drawing room, over to the old door, and she pulled it, rattled and shook it. No, it was locked fast, and the other mother had the key.

She looked around the room. It was so familiar – that was what made it feel so truly strange. Everything was exactly the same as she remembered: there was all her grandmother's strange-smelling furniture, there was the painting of the bowl of fruit (a bunch of grapes, two plums, a peach and an apple) hanging on the wall, there was the low wooden table with the lion's feet, and the empty fireplace which seemed to suck heat from the room.

But there was something else, something she did not remember seeing before. A ball of glass, up on the mantelpiece.

She went over to the fireplace, went up on tiptoes, and lifted it down. It was a snow-globe, with two little people in it. Coraline shook it and set the snow flying, white snow that glittered as it tumbled through the water.

Then she put the snow-globe back on the mantelpiece, and carried on looking for her true parents and for a way out.

She went out of the flat. Past the flashing-lights door, behind which the other Misses Spink and Forcible performed their show for ever, and set off into the woods.

Where Coraline came from, once you were through the patch of trees, you saw nothing but the meadow and the old tennis court. In this place, the woods went on further, the trees becoming cruder and less tree-like the further you went.

Pretty soon they seemed very approximate, like the idea of trees: a greyish-brown trunk below, a greenish splodge of something that might have been leaves above.

Coraline wondered if the other mother wasn't

interested in trees, or if she just hadn't bothered with this bit properly because nobody was expected to come out this far.

She kept walking.

And then the mist began.

It was not damp, like a normal fog or mist. It was not cold and it was not warm. It felt to Coraline like she was walking into nothing.

I'm an explorer, thought Coraline to herself. *And I need all the ways out of here that I can get. So I shall keep walking.*

The world she was walking through was a pale nothingness, like a blank sheet of paper or an enormous, empty white room. It had no temperature, no smell, no texture and no taste.

It certainly isn't mist, thought Coraline, although she did not know what it was. For a moment she wondered if she might have gone blind. But no, she could see herself, plain as day. There was no ground beneath her feet, just a misty, milky whiteness.

'And what do you think you're doing?' said a shape to one side of her.

It took a few moments for her eyes to focus on it properly. She thought it might be some kind of lion, at first, some distance away from her; and then she thought it might be a mouse, close beside her. And then she knew what it was.

'I'm exploring,' Coraline told the cat.

Its fur stood straight out from its body and its eyes were wide, while its tail was down and between its legs. It did not look a happy cat.

'Bad place,' said the cat. 'If you want to call it a place, which I don't. What are you doing here?'

'I'm exploring.'

'Nothing to find here,' said the cat. 'This is just the outside, the part of the place *she* hasn't bothered to create.'

'She?'

'The one who says she's your other mother,' said the cat.

'What *is* she?' asked Coraline.

The cat did not answer, just padded through the pale mist beside Coraline.

Something began to appear in front of them, something high and towering and dark.

'You were wrong!' she told the cat. 'There *is* something there!'

And then it took shape in the mist: a dark house, which loomed at them out of the formless whiteness.

'But that's –' said Coraline.

'The house you just left,' agreed the cat. 'Precisely.'

'Maybe I just got turned around in the mist,' said Coraline.

The cat curled the high tip of its tail into a question mark, and tipped its head on to one side. 'You might have done,' it said. 'I certainly would not. Wrong, indeed.'

'But how can you walk away from something and still come back to it?'

'Easy,' said the cat. 'Think of somebody walking around the world. You start out walking away from something and end up coming back to it.'

'Small world,' said Coraline.

'It's big enough for her,' said the cat. 'Spiders' webs only have to be large enough to catch flies.'

Coraline shivered.

'He said that she's fixing all the gates and the doors,' she told the cat, 'to keep you out.'

'She may *try*,' said the cat, unimpressed. 'Oh yes. She may try.' They were standing under a clump of trees now, beside the house. These trees looked much more likely. 'There's ways in and ways out of places like this that even *she* doesn't know about.'

'Did she make this place, then?' asked Coraline.

'Made it, found it, what's the difference?' asked the cat. 'Either way, she's had it a very long time. Hang on –' and it gave a shiver and a leap and before Coraline could blink the cat was sitting with its paw holding down a big black rat. 'It's not that I like rats at the best of times,' said the cat conversationally, as if nothing had happened, 'but the rats in this place are all spies for her. She uses them as her eyes and hands . . .' and with that the cat let the rat go.

It ran for almost a metre and then the cat, with one bound, was upon it, batting it hard with one sharp-clawed paw while holding it down with the other. 'I love this bit,' said the cat happily. 'Want to see me do that again?'

'No,' said Coraline. 'Why do you do it? You're torturing it.'

'Mm,' said the cat. It let the rat go.

The rat stumbled, dazed, for a few steps, then it began to run. With a blow of its paw, the cat knocked the rat into the air, and caught it in its mouth.

'Stop it!' said Coraline.

The cat dropped the rat between its two front paws. 'There are those,' it said with a sigh, in tones as smooth as oiled silk, 'who have suggested that the tendency of a cat to play with its prey is a merciful one – after all, it permits the occasional funny little running snack to escape, from time to time. How often does your dinner get to escape?'

And then it picked the rat up in its mouth and carried it off into the woods, behind a tree.

Coraline walked back into the house.

All was quiet and empty and deserted. Even

her footsteps on the carpeted floor seemed loud. Dust motes hung in a beam of sunlight.

At the far end of the hall was the mirror. She could see herself walking towards the mirror, looking, reflected, a little braver than she actually felt. There was nothing else there in the mirror. Just her, in the corridor.

A hand touched her shoulder, and she looked up. The other mother stared down at Coraline with big black-button eyes.

'Coraline, my darling,' she said. 'I thought we could play some games together this morning, now you're back from your walk. Hopscotch? Monopoly? Happy Families?'

'You weren't in the mirror,' said Coraline.

The other mother smiled. 'Mirrors,' she said, 'are never to be trusted. Now, what game shall we play?'

Coraline shook her head. 'I don't want to play with you,' she said. 'I want to go home and be with my real parents. I want you to let them go. To let us all go.'

The other mother shook her head, very slowly. 'Sharper than a serpent's tooth,' she said, 'is a daughter's ingratitude. Still, the proudest spirit can be broken, with love.' And her long white fingers waggled and caressed the air.

'I have no plans to love you,' said Coraline. 'No matter what. You can't make me love you.'

'Let's talk about it,' said the other mother, and she turned and walked into the sitting room. Coraline followed her.

The other mother sat down on the big sofa. She picked up a brown handbag from beside the sofa, and took out a white, rustling, paper bag from inside it.

She extended the hand with the paper bag in it to Coraline. 'Would you like one?' she asked politely.

Expecting it to be a toffee or a butterscotch ball, Coraline looked down. The bag was half filled with large shiny black beetles, crawling over each other in their efforts to get out of the bag.

'No,' said Coraline. 'I don't want one.'

'Suit yourself,' said her other mother. She carefully picked out a particularly large and black beetle, pulled off its legs (which she dropped, neatly, into a big glass ashtray on the small table beside the sofa), and popped the beetle into her mouth. She crunched it happily.

'Yum,' she said, and took another.

'You're sick,' said Coraline. 'Sick and evil and weird.'

'Is that any way to talk to your mother?' her

other mother asked, with her mouth full of black beetles.

'You aren't my mother,' said Coraline.

Her other mother ignored this. 'Now, I think you are a little overexcited, Coraline. Perhaps this afternoon we could do a little embroidery together, or some watercolour painting. Then dinner, and then, if you have been good, you may play with the rats a little before bed. And I shall read you a story and tuck you in, and kiss you goodnight.' Her long white fingers fluttered gently, like a tired butterfly, and Coraline shivered.

'No,' said Coraline.

The other mother sat on the sofa. Her mouth was set in a line; her lips were pursed. She popped another black beetle into her mouth, and then another, like someone with a bag of chocolate-covered raisins. Her big black-button eyes looked into Coraline's hazel eyes. Her shiny black hair twined and twisted about her neck and shoulders, as if it were blowing in some wind that Coraline could not touch or feel.

They stared at each other for over a minute. Then the other mother said, 'Manners!' She folded the white paper bag, carefully, so no black beetles could escape, and she placed it back in the shopping bag. Then she stood up, and up, and up: she seemed taller than Coraline remembered. She reached into her apron pocket and pulled out first the black door key, which she frowned at and tossed into her handbag, then a tiny silver-coloured key. She held it up triumphantly. 'There we are,' she said. 'This is for you, Coraline. For your own good. Because I love you. To teach you manners. Manners makyth man, after all.'

She pulled Coraline back into the hallway and advanced upon the mirror at the end of the hall. Then she pushed the tiny key into the fabric of the mirror, and she *twisted* it.

The mirror opened like a door, revealing a dark space behind it. 'You may come out when you've learned some manners,' said the other mother. 'And when you're ready to be a loving daughter.'

She picked Coraline up and pushed her into the dim space behind the mirror. A fragment of beetle was sticking to her lower lip, and there was no expression at all in her black-button eyes.

Then she swung the mirror-door closed, and left Coraline in darkness.

'She stole our hearts, and she stole our souls . . .'

CHAPTER 7

Somewhere inside her Coraline could feel a huge sob welling up. And then she stopped it, before it came out. She took a deep breath and let it go. She put out her hands to touch the space in which she was imprisoned. It was the size of a broom cupboard: tall enough to stand in or to sit in, not wide or deep enough to lie down in.

One wall was glass, and it felt cold to the touch.

She went around the tiny room a second time, running her hands over every surface that she could reach, feeling for doorknobs or switches or concealed catches – some kind of way out – and found nothing.

A spider scuttled over the back of her hand and she choked back a shriek. But apart from the spider she was alone in the cupboard, in the pitch dark.

And then her hand touched something that

felt for all the world like somebody's cheek and lips, small and cold, and a voice whispered in her ear, 'Hush! And shush! Say nothing, for the beldam might be listening!'

Coraline said nothing.

She felt a cold hand touch her face, fingers running over it like the gentle beat of a moth's wings.

Another voice, hesitant and so faint Coraline wondered if she were imagining it, said, 'Art thou – art thou *alive*?'

'Yes,' whispered Coraline.

'Poor child,' said the first voice.

'Who are you?' whispered Coraline.

'Names, names, names,' said another voice, all faraway and lost. 'The names are the first things to go, after the breath has gone, and the beating of the heart. We keep our memories longer than our names. I still keep pictures in my mind of my governess on some May morning, carrying my hoop and stick, and the morning sun behind her, and all the tulips bobbing in the breeze. But I have forgotten the name of my governess, and of the tulips too.'

'I don't think tulips have names,' said Coraline. 'They're just tulips.'

'Perhaps,' said the voice sadly. 'But I have always thought that these tulips must have had names. They were red, and orange-and-red, and red-and-orange-and-yellow, like the embers in the nursery fire of a winter's evening. I remember them.'

The voice sounded so sad that Coraline put out a hand to the place where it was coming from, and she found a cold hand, and she squeezed it tightly.

Her eyes were beginning to get used to the darkness. Now Coraline saw, or imagined she saw, three shapes, each as faint and pale as a moon in the daytime sky. They were the shapes of children about her own size. The cold hand squeezed her hand back. 'Thank you,' said the voice.

'Are you a girl?' asked Coraline. 'Or a boy?'

There was a pause. 'When I was small I wore skirts and my hair was long and curled,' it said doubtfully. 'But now that you ask, it does seem to me that one day they took my skirts and gave me britches and cut my hair.'

'Tain't something we give a mind to,' said the first of the voices.

'A boy, perhaps, then,' continued the one whose hand she was holding. 'I believe I was once a boy.' And it glowed a little more brightly in the darkness of the room behind the mirror.

'What happened to you all?' asked Coraline. 'How did you come here?'

'She left us here,' said one of the voices. 'She stole our hearts, and she stole our souls, and she took our lives away, and she left us here, and she forgot about us in the dark.'

'You poor things,' said Coraline. 'How long have you been here?'

'So very long a time,' said a voice.

'Aye. Time beyond reckoning,' said another voice.

'I walked through the scullery door,' said the voice of the one that thought it might be a boy, 'and I found myself back in the parlour. But *she* was waiting for me. She told me she was my other mamma, but I never saw my true mamma again.'

'Flee!' said the very first of the voices – another girl, Coraline fancied – 'Flee, while there's still air in your lungs and blood in your veins and warmth in your heart. Flee while you still have your mind and your soul.'

'I'm not running away,' said Coraline. 'She has my parents. I came to get them back.'

'Ah, but she'll keep you here while the days turn to dust and the leaves fall and the years pass one after the next like the tick-tick-ticking of a clock.'

'No,' said Coraline. 'She won't.'

There was silence then in the room behind the mirror.

'Peradventure,' said a voice in the darkness, 'if you could win your mama and your papa back from the beldam, you could also win free our souls.'

'Has she taken them?' asked Coraline, shocked.

'Aye. And hidden them.'

'That is why we could not leave here, when we died. She kept us, and she fed on us, until now we're nothing left of ourselves, only snakeskins and spider-husks. Find our secret hearts, young mistress.'

'And what will happen to you if I do?' asked Coraline.

The voices said nothing.

'And what is she going to do to me?' she said.

The pale figures pulsed faintly; she could imagine that they were nothing more than afterimages, like the glow left by a bright light in your eyes, after the lights go out.

'It doth not hurt,' whispered one faint voice.

'She will take your life and all you are and all you care'st for, and she will leave you with nothing but mist and fog. She'll take your joy. And one day you'll awake and your heart and your soul will have gone. A husk you'll be, a wisp you'll be, and a thing no more than a dream on waking, or a memory of something forgotten.'

'Hollow,' whispered the third voice. 'Hollow, hollow, hollow, hollow, hollow.'

'You must flee,' sighed a voice, faintly.

'I don't think so,' said Coraline. 'I tried running away, and it didn't work. She just took my parents. Can you tell me how to get out of this room?'

'If we knew then we would tell you.'

'Poor things,' said Coraline to herself.

She sat down. She took off her sweater and rolled it up and put it behind her head, as a pillow. 'She won't keep me in the dark for ever,' said Coraline. 'She brought me here to play games. "Games and challenges," the cat said. I'm not much of a challenge here in the dark.' She tried to get comfortable, twisting and bending herself to fit the cramped space behind the mirror. Her stomach rumbled. She ate her last apple, taking the tiniest bites, making it last as long as she could. When she had finished she was still hungry. Then an idea struck her, and she whispered, 'When she comes to let me out, why don't you three come with me?'

'We wish that we could,' they sighed to her, in their barely-there voices. 'But she has our hearts in her keeping. Now we belong to the dark and to the empty places. The light would shrivel us, and burn.'

'Oh,' said Coraline.

She closed her eyes, which made the darkness darker, and she rested her head on the rolled-up sweater, and she went to sleep. And as she fell asleep she thought she felt a ghost kiss her cheek, tenderly, and a small voice whisper into her ear, a voice so faint it was barely there at all, a gentle wispy nothing of a voice so hushed that Coraline could almost believe she was imagining it.

'Look through the stone,' it said to her. And then she slept.

The creature in the sac seemed horribly
unformed and unfinished . . .

CHAPTER 3

CHAPTER 8

The other mother looked healthier than before: there was a little blush to her cheeks, and her hair was wriggling like lazy snakes on a warm day. Her black-button eyes seemed as if they had been freshly polished.

She had pushed through the mirror as if she were walking through nothing more solid than water and had stared down at Coraline. Then she had opened the door with the little silver key. She picked Coraline up, just as Coraline's real mother had when Coraline was much younger, cradling the half-sleeping child as if she were a baby.

The other mother carried Coraline into the kitchen and put her down, very gently, upon the counter-top.

Coraline struggled to wake herself up, conscious only for the moment of having been cuddled and loved, and wanting more of it; then realising where she was, and who she was with.

'There, my sweet Coraline,' said her other mother. 'I came and fetched you out of the cupboard. You needed to be taught a lesson, but we temper our justice with mercy here, we love the sinner and we hate the sin. Now, if you will be a good child who loves her mother, be compliant and fair-spoken, you and I shall understand each other perfectly and we shall love each other perfectly as well.'

Coraline scratched the sleep-grit from her eyes.

'There were other children in there,' she said. 'Old ones, from a long time ago.'

'Were there?' said the other mother. She was bustling between the pans and the fridge, bringing out eggs and cheeses, butter and a slab of sliced pink bacon.

'Yes,' said Coraline. 'There were. I think you're planning to turn me into one of them. A dead shell.'

Her other mother smiled gently. With one hand she cracked the eggs into a bowl, with the other she whisked them and whirled them. Then she dropped a pat of butter into a frying pan, where it hissed and fizzled and spun as she sliced thin slices of cheese. She poured the melted butter and the cheese into the egg mixture, and whisked it some more.

'Now, I think you're being silly, dear,' said the

other mother. 'I love you. I will always love you. Nobody sensible believes in ghosts anyway. That's because they're all such liars. Smell the lovely breakfast I'm making for you.' She poured the yellow mixture into the pan. 'Cheese omelette. Your favourite.'

Coraline's mouth watered. 'You like games,' she said. 'That's what I've been told.'

The other mother's black eyes flashed. 'Everybody likes games,' was all she said.

'Yes,' said Coraline. She climbed down from the counter and sat at the kitchen table.

The bacon was sizzling and spitting under the grill. It smelled wonderful.

'Wouldn't you be happier if you won me, fair and square?' asked Coraline.

'Possibly,' said the other mother. She had a show of unconcernedness, but her fingers twitched and drummed and she licked her lips with her scarlet tongue. 'What exactly are you offering?'

'Me,' said Coraline, and she gripped her knees under the table, to stop them from shaking. 'If I lose I'll stay here with you for ever and I'll let you love me. I'll be a most dutiful daughter. I'll eat your food, and play Happy Families. And I'll let you sew your buttons into my eyes.'

Her other mother stared at her, black buttons

unblinking. 'That sounds very fine,' she said. 'And if you do not lose?'

'Then you let me go. You let everyone go – my real father and mother, the dead children, everyone you've trapped here.'

The other mother took the bacon from under the grill and put it on a plate. Then she slipped the cheese omelette from the pan on to the plate, flipping it as she did so, letting it fold itself into a perfect omelette shape.

She placed the breakfast plate in front of Coraline, along with a glass of freshly squeezed orange juice and a mug of frothy hot chocolate.

'Yes,' she said. 'I think I like this game. But what kind of game shall it be? A riddle game? A test of knowledge? Or of skill?'

'An exploring game,' suggested Coraline. 'A finding-things game.'

'And what is it you think you should be finding in this hide-and-go-seek game, Coraline Jones?'

Coraline hesitated. Then, 'My parents,' said Coraline. 'And the souls of the children behind the mirror.'

The other mother smiled at this, triumphantly, and Coraline wondered if she had made the right choice. Still, it was too late to change her mind now.

'A deal,' said the other mother. 'Now eat up

your breakfast, my sweet. Don't worry, it won't hurt you.'

Coraline stared at the breakfast, hating herself for giving in so easily; but she was starving.

'How do I know you'll keep your word?' asked Coraline.

'I swear it,' said the other mother. 'I swear it on my own mother's grave.'

'Does she have a grave?' asked Coraline.

'Oh yes,' said the other mother. 'I put her in there myself. And when I found her trying to crawl out, I put her back.'

'Swear on something else. So I can trust you to keep your word.'

'My right hand,' said the other mother, holding it up. She waggled the long fingers slowly, displaying the claw-like nails. 'I swear on that.'

Coraline shrugged. 'OK,' she said. 'It's a deal.' She ate the breakfast, trying not to wolf it down. She was hungrier than she had thought.

As she ate, the other mother stared at her. It was hard to read expressions into those black-button eyes, but Coraline thought that her other mother looked hungry, too.

She drank the orange juice, but even though she knew she would like it she could not bring herself to taste the hot chocolate.

'Where should I start looking?' asked Coraline.

'Where you wish,' said her other mother, as if she did not care at all.

Coraline looked at her, and Coraline thought hard. There was no point, she decided, in exploring the garden and the grounds: they didn't exist, they weren't real. There was no abandoned tennis court in the other mother's world, no bottomless well. All that was real was the house itself.

She looked around the kitchen. She opened the oven, peered into the freezer, poked into the salad compartment of the fridge. The other mother followed her about, looking at Coraline with a smirk always hovering at the edge of her lips.

'How big are souls anyway?' asked Coraline.

The other mother sat down at the kitchen table and leaned back against the wall, saying nothing. She picked at her teeth with a long crimson-varnished fingernail, then she tapped the finger gently, tap-tap-tap, against the polished black surface of her black-button eyes.

'Fine,' said Coraline. 'Don't tell me. I don't care. It doesn't matter if you help me or not. Everyone knows that a soul is the same size as a beach ball.'

She was hoping the other mother would say something like, 'Nonsense, they're the size of ripe onions – or suitcases – or grandfather clocks,' but the other mother simply smiled, and the tap-tap-tapping of her fingernail against her eye was as steady and relentless as the drip of water droplets from the tap into the sink. And then, Coraline realised, it *was* simply the noise of the water, and she was alone in the room.

Coraline shivered. She preferred the other mother to have a location: if she were nowhere, then she could be anywhere. And, after all, it is always easier to be afraid of something you cannot see. She put her hands into her pockets and her fingers closed around the reassuring shape of the stone with the hole in it. She pulled it out of her pocket, held it in front of her as if she were holding a gun, and walked out into the hall.

There was no sound but the tap-tap of the water dripping into the metal sink.

She glanced at the mirror at the end of the hall. For a moment it clouded over, and it seemed to her that faces swam in the glass, indistinct and shapeless, and then the faces were gone, and there was nothing in the mirror but a girl who was small for her age holding something that glowed gently, like a green coal.

Coraline looked down at her hand, surprised: it was just a pebble with a hole in it, a nondescript brown stone. Then she looked back into the mirror where the stone glimmered like an emerald. A trail

113

of green fire blew from the stone in the mirror, and drifted towards Coraline's bedroom.

'Hmm,' said Coraline.

She walked into the bedroom. The toys fluttered excitedly as she came in, as if they were pleased to see her, and a little tank rolled out of the toybox to greet her, its treads rolling over several other toys. It fell from the toybox on to the floor, tipping as it fell, and it lay on the carpet like a beetle on its back, grumbling and grinding its treads before Coraline picked it up and turned it over. The tank fled under the bed in embarrassment.

Coraline looked around the room.

She looked in the cupboards and the drawers. Then she picked up one end of the toybox and tipped all the toys in it out on to the carpet, where they grumbled and stretched and wiggled awkwardly free of each other. A grey marble rolled across the floor and clicked against the wall. None of the toys looked particularly soul-like, she thought. She picked up and examined a silver charm-bracelet from which hung tiny animal charms which chased each other around the perimeter of the bracelet, the fox never catching the rabbit, the bear never gaining on the fox.

Coraline opened her hand and looked at the stone with the hole in it, hoping for a clue but not finding one. Most of the toys that had been in the toybox had now crawled away to hide under the bed, and the few toys that were left (a green plastic soldier, the glass marble, a vivid pink yo-yo, and such) were the kind of things you find in the bottoms of toyboxes in the real world: forgotten objects, abandoned and unloved.

She was about to leave and look elsewhere. And then she remembered a voice in the darkness, a gentle whispering voice, and what it had told her to do. She raised the stone with the hole in it, and held it in front of her right eye. She closed her left eye and looked at the room through the hole in the stone.

Through the stone, the world was grey and colourless, like a pencil drawing. Everything in it was grey – no, not quite everything. Something glinted on the floor, something the colour of an ember in a nursery fireplace, the colour of a scarlet-and-orange tulip nodding in the May sun. Coraline reached out her left hand, scared that if she took her eye off it it would vanish, and she fumbled for the burning thing.

Her fingers closed about something smooth and cool. She snatched it up, and then lowered the stone with the hole in it from her eye and looked down. The grey glass marble from the bottom of the toybox sat, dully, in the pink palm of her hand. She raised the stone to her eye once more, and looked through it at the marble. Once again the marble burned and flickered with a red fire.

A voice whispered in her mind, 'Indeed, lady, it comes to me that I certainly *was* a boy, now I do think on it. Oh, but you must hurry. There are two of us still to find, and the beldam is already angry with you for uncovering me.'

If I'm going to do this, thought Coraline, *I'm not going to do it in her clothes.* She changed back into her pyjamas and her dressing gown and her slippers, leaving the grey sweater and the black jeans neatly folded up on the bed, the orange boots on the floor by the toy box.

She put the marble into her dressing-gown pocket and walked out into the hall.

Something stung her face and hands like sand blowing on a beach on a windy day. She covered her eyes, and pushed forward.

The sand-stings got worse, and it got harder and harder to walk, as if she were pushing into the wind on a particularly blustery day. It was a vicious wind, and a cold one.

She took a step backwards, the way she had come.

'Oh, keep going,' whispered a ghost-voice in her ear. 'For the beldam is angry.'

She stepped forward in the hallway, into another gust of wind, which stung her cheeks and face with invisible sand, sharp as needles, sharp as glass.

'Play fair,' shouted Coraline, into the wind.

There was no reply, but the wind whipped about her one more time, petulantly, and then it dropped away, and was gone. As she passed the kitchen Coraline could hear, in the sudden silence, the drip-drip of the water from the leaking tap, or perhaps the other mother's long fingernails tapping impatiently against the table. Coraline resisted the urge to look.

In a couple of strides she reached the front door, and she walked outside.

Coraline went down the steps and around the house until she reached the other Miss Spink and Miss Forcible's flat. The lamps around the door were flickering on and off almost randomly now, spelling out no words that Coraline could under-stand. The door was closed. She was afraid it was locked, and she pushed on it with all her strength. First it stuck, then suddenly it gave, and, with a jerk, Coraline stumbled into the dark room beyond.

Coraline closed one hand around the stone with the hole in it and walked forward into black-ness. She expected to find a curtained anteroom, but there was nothing there. The room was dark. The theatre was empty. She moved ahead cautiously. Something rustled above her. She looked up into a deeper darkness, and as she did so her feet knocked against something. She reached down, picked up a torch, and clicked it on, sweeping the beam around the room.

The theatre was derelict and abandoned. Chairs were broken on the floor, and old, dusty spiders' webs draped the walls and hung from the rotten wood and the decomposing velvet hangings.

Something rustled once again. Coraline directed her light beam upwards, towards the ceiling. There were things up there, hairless, jellyish. She thought they might once have had faces, might even once have been dogs; but no dogs had wings like bats, or could hang, like spiders, like bats, upside-down.

The light startled the creatures, and one of them took to the air, its wings whirring heavily through the dust. Coraline ducked as it swooped close to her. It came to rest on a far wall, and it began to clamber, upside-down, back to the nest of the dog-bats upon the ceiling.

Coraline raised the stone to her eye and she scanned the room through it, looking for something that glowed or glinted, a telltale sign that somewhere in this room was another hidden soul. She ran the beam of the torch about the room as she searched, the thick dust in the air making the light beam seem almost solid.

There was something up on the back wall behind the ruined stage. It was greyish-white, twice the size of

Coraline herself, and it was stuck to the back wall like a slug. Coraline took a deep breath. 'I'm not afraid,' she told herself. 'I'm not.' She did not believe herself, but she scrambled on to the old stage, fingers sinking into the rotting wood as she pulled herself up.

As she got closer to the thing on the wall, she saw that it was some kind of a sac, like a spider's egg-case. It twitched in the light beam. Inside the sac was something that looked like a person, but a person with two heads, with twice as many arms and legs as it should have.

The creature in the sac seemed horribly unformed and unfinished, as if two Plasticine people had been warmed and rolled together, squashed and pressed into one thing.

Coraline hesitated. She did not want to approach the thing. The dog-bats dropped, one by one, from the ceiling, and began to circle the room, coming close to her but never touching her.

Perhaps there are no souls hidden in here, she thought. *Perhaps I can just leave and go somewhere else.* She took a last look through the hole in the stone: the abandoned theatre was still a bleak grey, but now there was a brown glow, as rich and bright as polished cherrywood, coming from inside the sac. Whatever was glowing was being held in one of the hands of the thing on the wall.

Coraline walked slowly across the damp stage, trying to make as little noise as she could, afraid that, if she disturbed the thing in the sac, it would open its eyes, and see her, and then . . .

But there was nothing that she could think of that was as scary as having it look at her. Her heart pounded in her chest. She took another step forward.

She had never been so scared, but still she walked forward until she reached the sac. Then she pushed her hand into the sticky, clinging whiteness of the stuff on the wall. It crackled softly, like a tiny fire, as she pushed, and it clung to her skin and clothes like a spider's web clings, like white candy-floss. She pushed her hand into it, and she reached upward until she touched a cold hand, which was, she could feel, closed around another glass marble. The creature's skin felt slippery, as if it had been covered in jelly. Coraline tugged at the marble.

At first nothing happened; it was held tight in the creature's grasp. Then, one by one, the fingers loosened their grip, and the marble slipped into her hand. She pulled her arm back through the sticky webbing, relieved that the thing's eyes had not opened. She shone the light on its faces: they resembled, she decided, the younger versions of Miss Spink and Miss Forcible, but twisted and squeezed together, like two lumps of wax that had melted and melded together into one ghastly object.

Without warning, one of the creature's hands made a grab for Coraline's arm. Its fingernails scraped her skin, but it was too slippery to grip, and Coraline pulled away successfully. And then the eyes opened – four black buttons glinting and staring down at her – and two voices that sounded like no voice that Coraline had ever heard began to speak to her. One of them wailed and whispered, the other buzzed like a fat and angry bluebottle at a windowpane, but the voices said, as one person, 'Thief! Give it back! Stop! Thief!'

The air became alive with dog-bats. Coraline began to back away. She realised then that, terrifying though the thing on the wall was, the thing that had once been the other Misses Spink and Forcible, it was attached to the wall by its web, encased in its cocoon. It could not follow her.

The dog-bats flapped and fluttered about her, but they did nothing to hurt Coraline. She climbed down from the stage and shone the torch about the old theatre looking for the way out.

'Flee, miss,' wailed a girl's voice in her head. 'Flee, now. You have two of us. Flee this place while your blood still flows.'

Coraline dropped the marble into her pocket beside the other. She spotted the door, ran to it, and pulled on it until it opened.

'You'll need this to get in.'

CHAPTER 9

Outside, the world had become a formless, swirling mist with no shapes or shadows behind it, while the house itself seemed to have twisted and stretched. It appeared to Coraline that it was crouching and staring down at her, as if it were not really a house but only the idea of a house – and the person who had had the idea, she was certain, was not a good person. There was sticky web-stuff clinging to her arm, and she wiped it off as best she could. The grey windows of the house slanted at strange angles.

The other mother was waiting for her, standing on the grass with her arms folded. Her black-button eyes were expressionless, but her lips were pressed tightly together in a cold fury.

When she saw Coraline she reached out one long white hand, and she crooked a finger.

125

Coraline walked towards her. The other mother said nothing.

'I've found two,' said Coraline. 'One soul still to go.'

The expression on the other mother's face did not change. She might not have heard what Coraline said.

'Well, I just thought you'd want to know,' said Coraline.

'Thank you, Coraline,' said the other mother coldly, and her voice did not just come from her mouth. It came from the mist, and the fog, and the house, and the sky. She said, 'You know that I love you.'

And, despite herself, Coraline nodded. It was true: the other mother loved her. But she loved Coraline as a miser loves money, or a dragon loves its gold. In the other mother's button eyes, Coraline knew that she was a possession, nothing more. A tolerated pet, whose behaviour was no longer amusing.

'I don't want your love,' said Coraline. 'I don't want anything from you.'

'Not even a helping hand?' asked the other mother. 'You have been doing so well, after all. I thought you might want a little hint, to help you with the rest of your treasure hunt.'

'I'm doing fine on my own,' said Coraline.

'Yes,' said the other mother. 'But if you wanted to get into the flat in the front – the empty one – to look around, you would find the door locked, and then where would you be?'

'Oh.' Coraline pondered this for a moment. Then she said, 'Is there a key?'

The other mother stood there in the paper-grey fog of the flattening world. Her black hair drifted about her head, as if it had a mind and a purpose all of its own. She coughed, suddenly, in the back of her throat, and then she opened her mouth.

The other mother reached up her hand and removed a small, brass, front-door key from her tongue.

'Here,' she said. 'You'll need this to get in.'

She tossed the key, casually, towards Coraline, who caught it, one-handed, before she could think about whether she wanted it or not. The key was still slightly damp.

A chill wind blew about them, and Coraline shivered and looked away. When she looked back she was alone.

Uncertainly, she walked round to the front of the house and stood in front of the door to the empty flat. Like all the doors, it was painted bright green.

'She does not mean you well,' whispered a ghost-voice in her ear. 'We do not believe that she would help you. It must be a trick.'

Coraline said, 'Yes, you're right, I expect.' Then she put the key in the lock, and turned it.

Silently the door swung open, and silently Coraline walked inside.

The flat had walls the colour of old milk. The wooden boards of the floor were uncarpeted and dusty with the marks and patterns of old carpets and rugs on them.

There was no furniture in there, only places where furniture had once been. Nothing decorated the walls; there were discoloured rectangles on the walls to show where paintings or photographs had once hung. It was so silent that Coraline imagined that she could hear the motes of dust drifting through the air.

She found herself to be quite worried that something would jump out at her, so she began to whistle. She thought it might make it harder for things to jump out at her, if she was whistling.

First she walked through the empty kitchen. Then she walked through an empty bathroom, containing only a cast-iron bath, and, in the bath, a dead spider the size of a small cat. The last room she looked at had, she supposed, once been a bedroom;

she could imagine that the rectangular dust-shadow on the floorboards had once been a bed. Then she saw something, and smiled, grimly. Set into the floorboards was a large metal ring. Coraline knelt and took the cold ring in her hands, and she tugged upward, as hard as she could.

Terribly slowly, stiffly, heavily, a hinged square of floor lifted: it was a trapdoor. It lifted, and through the opening Coraline could see only darkness. She reached down, and her hand found a cold switch. She flicked it without much hope that it would work, but somewhere below her a bulb lit, and a thin yellow light came up from the hole in the floor. She could see steps, heading down, but nothing else.

Coraline put her hand into her pocket and took out the stone with the hole in it. She looked through it at the cellar but saw nothing. She put the stone back into her pocket.

Up through the hole in the floor came the smell of damp clay, and something else, an acrid tang like sour vinegar.

Coraline let herself down into the hole, looking nervously at the trapdoor. It was so heavy that if it fell she was sure she would be trapped down in the darkness for ever. She put up a hand and touched it, but it stayed in position. And then she turned towards the darkness below, and she walked down the steps. Set into the wall at the bottom of the steps was another light switch, metal and rusting. She pushed it until it clicked down, and a naked bulb hanging from a wire from the low ceiling came on. It did not give out enough light even for Coraline to make out the things that had been painted on to the flaking cellar walls. The paintings seemed crude. There were eyes, she could see that, and things that might have been grapes. And other things, below them. Coraline could not be sure that they were paintings of people.

There was a pile of rubbish in one corner of the room: cardboard boxes filled with mildewed papers, and decaying curtains in a heap beside them.

Coraline's slippers crunched across the cement floor. The bad smell was worse now. She was ready to turn and leave, when she saw the foot sticking out from beneath the pile of curtains.

She took a deep breath (the smells of sour wine and mouldy bread filled her head) and pulled away the damp cloth to reveal something more or less the size and shape of a person.

In that dim light, it took her several seconds to recognise it for what it was: the thing was pale and swollen, like a grub, with thin, stick-like arms and feet. It had almost no features on its face, which had puffed and swollen like risen bread dough.

The thing had two large black buttons where its eyes should have been.

Coraline made a noise, a sound of revulsion and horror, and, as if it had heard her and awakened, the thing began to sit up. Coraline stood there, frozen. The thing turned its head until both its black-button eyes were pointed straight at her. A mouth opened in the mouthless face, strands of pale stuff sticking to the lips, and a voice that no longer even faintly resembled her father's whispered, 'Coraline.'

'Well,' said Coraline to the thing that had once been her other father, 'at least you didn't jump out at me.'

The creature's twig-like hands moved to its face and pushed the pale clay about, making something like a nose. It said nothing.

'I'm looking for my parents,' said Coraline. 'Or a stolen soul, from one of the other children. Are they down here?'

'There is nothing down here,' said the pale thing, indistinctly. 'Nothing but dust and damp and forgetting.' The thing was white, and huge, and swollen. Monstrous, thought Coraline, but also miserable. She raised the stone with the hole in it to her eye, and looked through it. Nothing. The pale thing was telling her the truth.

'Poor thing,' she said. 'I bet she made you come down here as a punishment for telling me too much.'

The thing hesitated, then it nodded. Coraline wondered how she could ever have imagined that this grub-like thing resembled her father.

'I'm so sorry,' she said.

'She's not best pleased,' said the thing that was once the other father. 'Not best pleased at all. You've put her quite out of sorts. And when she gets out of sorts, she takes it out on everybody else. It's her way.'

Coraline patted its hairless head. Its skin was tacky, like warm bread dough. 'Poor thing,' she said. 'You're just a thing she made and then threw away.'

The thing nodded vigorously; as it nodded, the left button-eye fell off and clattered on to the concrete floor. The thing looked around vacantly with its one eye, as if it had lost her. Finally it saw her, and, as if making a great effort, it opened its mouth once more and said in a wet, urgent voice, 'Run, child. Leave this place. She wants me to hurt you, to keep you here for ever, so that you can never finish the game, and she will win. She is pushing me so hard to hurt you. I cannot fight her.'

'You *can*,' said Coraline. 'Be brave.'

She looked around: the thing that had once

been the other father was between her and the steps up and out of the cellar. She started edging along the wall, heading towards the steps. The thing twisted bonelessly until its one eye was again facing her. It seemed to be getting bigger now, and more awake. 'Alas,' it said. 'I cannot.'

And it lunged across the cellar towards her then, its toothless mouth opened wide.

Coraline had a single heartbeat in which to react. She could only think of two things to do. Either she could scream, and try to run away, and be chased around a badly lit cellar by the huge grubthing – be chased until it caught her. Or she could do something else.

So she did something else.

As the thing reached her, Coraline put out her hand and closed it around the thing's remaining button-eye, and she tugged, as hard as she knew how.

For a moment nothing happened. Then the button came away and flew from her hand, clicking against the brickwork before it fell to the cellar floor.

The thing froze in place. It threw its pale head back blindly, and opened its mouth horribly wide, and it roared its anger and frustration. Then, all in a rush, the thing swept towards the place where Coraline had been standing.

But Coraline was not standing there any longer. She was already tiptoeing, as quietly as she could, up the steps that would take her away from the dim cellar with the crude paintings on the walls. She could not take her eyes from the floor beneath her, though, across which a pale thing flopped and writhed, hunting for her. Then, as if it was being told what to do, the creature stopped moving, and its blind head tipped to one side.

It's listening for me, thought Coraline. I *must be extra quiet*. She took another step up and her foot slipped on the step, and the thing heard her.

Its head tipped towards her. For a moment it swayed and seemed to be gathering its wits. Then, fast as a serpent, it slithered for the steps, and began to flow up them, towards her. Coraline turned and ran wildly up the last half-dozen steps, and she pushed herself up and on to the floor of the dusty bedroom. Without pausing, she pulled the heavy trapdoor towards her, and let go of it. It crashed down with a thump just as something large banged against it. The trapdoor shook and rattled in the floor, but it stayed where it was.

Coraline took a deep breath. If there had been any furniture in that flat, even a chair, she would have pulled it on to the trapdoor, but there was nothing.

She walked out of that flat as fast as she could, without actually ever running, and she locked the front door behind her. She left the door-key under the mat. Then she walked down on to the drive.

Coraline had half expected that the other mother would be standing there waiting for her to come out, but the world was silent and empty.

Coraline wanted to go home.

She hugged herself, and told herself that she was brave, and she almost believed herself, and then she walked around to the side of the house, in the grey mist that wasn't a mist, and she made for the stairs, to go up.

The cat lifted its paw from the marble, which
rolled towards Coraline.

CHAPTER 10

Coraline walked up the steps outside the building to the topmost flat where, in her world, the crazy old man upstairs lived. She had gone up there once with her real mother, when her mother was collecting for charity. They had stood in the open doorway, waiting for the crazy old man with the big moustache to find the envelope that Coraline's mother had left, and the flat had smelled of strange foods and pipe tobacco and odd, sharp, cheesy-smelling things which Coraline could not name. She had not wanted to go any further inside than that.

'I'm an explorer,' said Coraline out loud, but her words sounded muffled and dead on the misty air. She had made it out of the cellar, hadn't she?

And she had. But if there was one thing that Coraline was certain of, it was that this flat would be worse.

She reached the top of the steps. The topmost flat had once been the attic of the house, but that was long ago.

She knocked on the green-painted door. It swung open, and she walked in.

> *We have eyes and we have nerveses*
> *We have tails, we have teeth,*
> *You'll all get what you deserveses*
> *When we rise from underneath,*

whispered a dozen or more tiny voices, in that dark flat with the roof so low where it met the walls that Coraline could almost reach up and touch it.

Red eyes stared at her. Little pink feet scurried away as she came close. Darker shadows slipped through the shadows at the edges of things.

It smelt much worse in here than in the real crazy old man upstairs's flat. That smelled of food (unpleasant food, to Coraline's mind, but she knew that was a matter of taste: she did not like spices, herbs or exotic things). This place smelled as if all the exotic foods in the world had been left out to go rotten.

'Little girl,' said a rustling voice in a far room.

'Yes,' said Coraline. I'm *not frightened*, she told herself, and as she thought it she knew that it was true. There was nothing here that frightened her. These things – even the thing in the cellar – were illusions, things made by the other mother in a ghastly parody of the real people and real things on the other end of the corridor. She couldn't truly make anything, decided Coraline. She could only twist and copy and distort things that already existed.

And then Coraline found herself wondering why the other mother would have placed a snow-globe on the drawing-room mantelpiece; a place that, in her world, was quite bare.

And once she had asked herself the question, she began to understand the answer.

Then the voice came again, and her train of thought was gone.

'Come here, little girl. I know what you want, little girl.' It was a rustling voice, scratchy and dry. It made Coraline think of some kind of enormous dead insect. Which was silly, she knew. How could a dead thing, especially a dead insect, have a voice?

She walked through several rooms with low, slanting ceilings until she came to the final room. It was a bedroom, and the other crazy old man upstairs sat at the far end of the room, in the near-darkness, bundled up in his coat and hat. As Coraline entered he began to talk. 'Nothing's changed, little girl,' he said, his voice sounding like the noise dry leaves make as they rustle across a pavement. 'And what if you do everything you swore you would? What then? Nothing's changed. You'll go home. You'll be bored. You'll be ignored. No one will listen to you, not really listen to you. You're too clever and too quiet for them to understand. They don't even get your name right.

'Stay here with us,' said the voice from the figure at the end of the room. 'We will listen to you and play with you and laugh with you. Your other mother will build whole worlds for you to explore, and tear them down every night when you are done. Every day will be better and brighter than the one that went before. Remember the toybox? How much better would a world be built just like that, and all for you?'

'And will there be grey, wet days where I just don't know what to do and there's nothing to read or to watch and nowhere to go and the day drags on for ever?' asked Coraline.

From the shadows, the man said, 'Never.'

'And will there be awful meals, with food made from recipes, with garlic and tarragon and broad beans in?' asked Coraline.

'Every meal will be a thing of joy,' whispered the voice from under the old man's hat. 'Nothing will pass your lips that does not entirely delight you.'

'And could I have Day-Glo green gloves to wear, and yellow wellington boots in the shape of frogs?' asked Coraline.

'Frogs, ducks, rhinos, octopuses – whatever you desire. The world will be built new for you every morning. If you stay here, you can have whatever you want.'

Coraline sighed. 'You really don't understand, do you?' she said. 'I don't *want* whatever I want. Nobody does. Not really. What kind of fun would it be if I just got everything I ever wanted? Just like that, and it didn't *mean* anything. What then?'

'I don't understand,' said the whispery voice.

'Of course you don't understand,' she said, raising the stone with the hole in it to her eye. 'You're just a bad copy she made of the crazy old man upstairs.'

There was a glow coming from the raincoat of the man, at about chest height. Through the hole in the stone the glow twinkled and shone blue-white as any star. She wished she had a stick or something to poke him with; she had no wish to get any closer to the shadowy man at the end of the room.

'Not even that any more,' said the dead, whispery voice.

Coraline took a step closer to the man, and he fell apart. Black rats leapt from the sleeves and from under the coat and hat, a score or more of them, red eyes shining in the dark. They chittered and they fled. The coat fluttered and fell heavily to the floor. The hat rolled into one corner of the room.

Coraline reached out her hand and pulled the coat open. It was empty, although it was greasy to the touch. There was no sign of the final glass marble in it. She scanned the room, squinting through the hole in the stone, and caught sight of something that twinkled and burned like a star, at floor level, by the doorway. It was being carried in the forepaws of the largest black rat. As she looked, it slipped away.

The other rats watched her from the corners of the room as she ran after it.

Now, rats can run faster than people, especially over short distances. But a large black rat holding a marble in its two front paws is no match for a determined girl (even if she is small for her age) moving at a run. Smaller black rats ran back and forth across her path, trying to distract her, but she ignored them all, keeping her eyes fixed on the one with the marble, who was heading straight out of the flat, towards the front door.

They reached the steps on the outside of the building.

Coraline had time to observe that the house itself was continuing to change, becoming less distinct, and flattening out, even as she raced down the stairs. It reminded her of a photograph of a house now, not the thing itself. Then she was simply racing pell-mell down the steps in pursuit of the rat, with no room in her mind for anything else, certain she was gaining on it. She was running fast – too fast, she discovered, as she came to the bottom of one flight of steps, and her foot skidded and twisted and she went crashing on to the concrete landing.

Her left knee was scraped and skinned, and the palm of one hand she had thrown out to stop herself was a mess of scraped skin and grit. It hurt a little, and it would, she knew, soon hurt much more. She picked the grit out of the palm and climbed to her feet and, as fast as she could, knowing that she had lost and it was already too late, she went down the final set of steps to ground level.

She looked around for the rat, but it was gone, and the marble with it.

Her hand stung where the skin had been scraped, and there was blood trickling down her ripped pyjama-leg from her knee. It was as bad as the summer that her mother had taken the training wheels off Coraline's bicycle; but then, back then, in with all the cuts and scrapes (her knees had had scabs on top of scabs) she had a feeling of achievement. She was learning something, doing something she had not known how to do before. Now she felt nothing but cold loss. She had failed the ghost-children. She had failed her parents. She had failed herself, failed everything.

She closed her eyes and wished that the earth would swallow her up.

There was a cough.

She opened her eyes, and saw the rat. It was lying on the brick path at the bottom of the steps, with a surprised look on its face – which was now several centimetres away from the rest of it. Its whiskers were stiff, its eyes were wide open, its teeth visible and yellow and sharp. A collar of wet blood glistened at its neck.

Beside the decapitated rat, a smug expression on its face, was the black cat. It rested one paw on the grey glass marble.

'I think I once mentioned,' said the cat, 'that I don't like rats at the best of times. It looked like you needed this one, however. I hope you don't mind my getting involved.'

'I think,' said Coraline, trying to catch her breath, 'I think you may . . . have said . . . something of the sort.'

The cat lifted its paw from the marble, which rolled towards Coraline. She picked it up. In her mind, a final voice whispered to her, urgently.

'She has lied to you. She will never give you up, now she has you. She will no more give any of us up than she can change her nature.' The hairs on the back of Coraline's neck prickled, and Coraline knew that the girl's voice told the truth. She put the marble in her dressing-gown pocket with the others.

She had all three marbles, now.

All she needed to do was to find her parents.

And, Coraline realised, that was easy. She knew exactly where her parents were. If she had stopped to think, she might have known where they were all along. The other mother could not create. She could only transform, and twist, and change.

And the mantelpiece in the drawing room back home was quite empty. But, knowing that, she knew something else, as well.

'The other mother. She plans to break her promise. She won't let us go,' said Coraline.

'I wouldn't put it past her,' admitted the cat. 'Like I said, there's no guarantee she'll play fair.' And then he raised his head. 'Hello . . . did you see that?'

'What?'

'Look behind you,' said the cat.

The house had flattened out even more. It no longer looked like a photograph – more like a drawing, a crude, charcoal scribble of a house drawn on grey paper.

'Whatever's happening,' said Coraline, 'thank you for helping with the rat. I suppose I'm almost there, aren't I? So you go off into the mist or wherever you go, and I'll, well, I hope I get to see you at home. If she lets me go home.'

The cat's fur was on end, and its tail was bristling like a chimney-sweep's brush.

'What's wrong?' asked Coraline.

'They've gone,' said the cat. 'They aren't there any more. The ways in and out of this place. They just went flat.'

'Is that bad?'

The cat lowered its tail, swishing it from side to side angrily. It made a low growling noise in the back of its throat. It walked in a circle, until it was facing away from Coraline, and then it began to walk backwards, stiffly, one step at a time, until it was pushing up against Coraline's leg. She put down a hand to stroke it, and could feel how hard its heart was beating. It was trembling, like a dead leaf in a storm.

'You'll be fine,' said Coraline. 'Everything's going to be fine. I'll take you home.'

The cat said nothing.

'Come on, cat,' said Coraline. She took a step back towards the steps, but the cat stayed where it was, looking miserable and, oddly, much smaller.

'If the only way out is past her,' said Coraline, 'then that's the way we're going to go.' She went back to the cat, bent down and picked it up. The cat did not resist. It simply trembled. She supported its bottom with one hand and rested its front legs on her shoulder. The cat was heavy, but not too heavy to carry. It licked at the palm of her hand, where the blood from the scrape was welling up.

Coraline walked up the steps one at a time, heading back to her own flat. She was aware of the marbles clicking in her pocket, aware of the stone with the hole in it, aware of the cat pressing itself against her.

She got to her front door – now just a small-child's scrawl of a door – and she pushed her hand against it, half expecting that her hand would rip through it, revealing nothing behind it but black-ness and a scattering of stars.

But the door swung open, and Coraline went through.

Her hair writhed and twined about her head, and
her teeth were sharp as knives . . .

CHAPTER 11

Once inside, in her flat, or rather, in the flat that
was not hers, Coraline was pleased to see that it had
not transformed into the empty drawing that the
rest of the house seemed to have become. It had
depth and shadows, and someone who stood in the
shadows waiting for Coraline to return.

'So you're back,' said the other mother. She
did not sound pleased. 'And you brought vermin
with you.'

'No,' said Coraline. 'I brought a friend.' She
could feel the cat stiffening under her hands, as if it
were anxious to be away. Coraline wanted to hold
on to it like a teddy bear, for reassurance, but she
knew that cats hate to be squeezed, and she
suspected that frightened cats were liable to bite
and scratch if provoked in any way, even if they
were on your side.

'You know I love you,' said the other mother, flatly.

'You have a very funny way of showing it,' said Coraline. She walked down the hallway, then turned into the drawing room, steady step by steady step, pretending that she could not feel the other mother's blank black eyes on her back. Her grandmother's formal furniture was still there, and the painting on the wall of the strange fruit (but now the fruit in the painting had been eaten, and all that remained in the bowl was the browning core of an apple, several plum and peach stones, and the stem of what had formerly been a bunch of grapes). The lion-pawed table raked the carpet with its clawed wooden feet, as if it were impatient for something. At the end of the room, in the corner, stood the wooden door, which had once, in another place, opened on to a plain brick wall. Coraline tried not to stare at it. The window showed nothing but mist.

This was it, Coraline knew. The moment of truth. The unravelling time.

The other mother had followed her in. Now she stood in the centre of the room, between Coraline and the mantelpiece, and looked down at Coraline with black-button eyes. It was funny, Coraline thought. The other mother did not look anything at all like her own mother. She wondered how she had ever been deceived into imagining a resemblance. The other mother was huge – her head almost brushed the ceiling of the room – and very pale, the colour of a spider's belly. Her hair writhed and twined about her head, and her teeth were sharp as knives . . .

'Well?' said the other mother, sharply. 'Where are they?'

Coraline leaned against an armchair, adjusted the cat with her left hand, put her right hand into her pocket, and pulled out the three glass marbles. They were a frosted grey, and they clinked together in the palm of her hand. The other mother reached her white fingers out for them, but Coraline slipped them back into her pocket. She knew it was true, then. The other mother had no intention of letting her go, or of keeping her word. It had been an entertainment, and nothing more. 'Hold on,' she said. 'We aren't finished yet, are we?'

The other mother looked daggers, but she smiled sweetly. 'No,' she said. 'I suppose not. After all, you still need to find your parents, don't you?'

'Yes,' said Coraline. I *must not look at the mantelpiece*, she thought. I *must not even think about it*.

'Well?' said the other mother. 'Produce them. Would you like to look in the cellar again? I have some other interesting things hidden down there, you know.'

'No,' said Coraline. 'I know where my parents are.' The cat was heavy in her arms. She moved it forward, unhooking its claws from her shoulder as she did so.

'Where?'

'It stands to reason,' said Coraline. 'I've looked everywhere you'd hide them. They aren't in the house.'

The other mother stood very still, giving nothing away, lips tightly closed. She might have been a wax statue. Even her hair had stopped moving.

'So,' Coraline continued, both hands wrapped firmly around the black cat, 'I know where they have to be. You've hidden them in the passageway between the houses, haven't you? They are behind that door.' She nodded her head towards the door in the corner.

The other mother remained statue-still, but a hint of a smile crept back on to her face. 'Oh, they are, are they?'

'Why don't you open it?' said Coraline. 'They'll be there, all right.'

It was her only way home, she knew. But it all depended on the other mother needing to gloat, needing not only to win but to show that she had won.

The other mother reached her hand slowly into her apron pocket and produced the black iron key. The cat stirred uncomfortably in Coraline's arms, as if it wanted to get down. *Just stay there for a few moments longer*, she thought at it, wondering if it could hear her. *I'll get us both home. I said I would. I promise.* She felt the cat relax ever-so-slightly in her arms.

The other mother walked over to the door and pushed the key into the lock.

She turned the key.

Coraline heard the mechanism clunk heavily. She was already starting, as quietly as she could, step by step, to back away towards the mantelpiece.

The other mother pushed down on the door handle and pulled open the door, revealing a corridor behind it, dark and empty. 'There,' she said, waving her hands at the corridor. The expression of delight on her face was a very bad thing to see. 'You're wrong! You *don't* know where your parents are, do you? They aren't there.' She turned and looked at Coraline. 'Now,' she said, 'you're going to stay here for ever and always.'

'No,' said Coraline. 'I'm not.' And, hard as she could, she threw the black cat towards the other mother. It yowled and landed on the other mother's head, claws flailing, teeth bared, fierce and angry. Fur on end, it looked half again as big as it was in real life.

Without waiting to see what would happen, Coraline reached up to the mantelpiece, closed her hand around the snow-globe, then pushed it deep into the pocket of her dressing gown.

The cat made a deep, ululating yowl and sank its teeth into the other mother's cheek. She was flailing at it. Blood ran from the cuts on her white face – not red blood, but a deep, tarry black stuff. Coraline ran for the door.

She pulled the key out of the lock.

'Leave her! Come on!' she shouted to the cat. It hissed, and swiped its scalpel-sharp claws at the other mother's face in one wild rake which left black ooze trickling from several gashes on her nose. Then it sprang down towards Coraline. 'Quickly!' she said. The cat ran towards her, and they both stepped into the dark corridor.

It was colder in the corridor, like stepping down into a cellar on a warm day. The cat hesitated for a moment, then, seeing the other mother was coming towards them, it ran to Coraline and stopped by her legs.

Coraline began to pull the door closed.

It was heavier than she imagined a door could be, and pulling it closed was like trying to close a door against a high wind. And then she felt something from the other side starting to pull against her.

Shut! she thought. Then she said, out loud, 'Come on, *please*.' And she felt the door begin to move, to pull closed, to give against the phantom wind.

Suddenly she was aware of other people in the corridor with her. She could not turn her head to look at them, but she knew them without having to look. 'Help me, please,' she said. 'All of you.'

The other people in the corridor – three children, two adults – were somehow too insubstantial to touch the door. But their hands closed about hers, as she pulled on the big iron door handle, and suddenly she felt strong.

'Never let up, miss! Hold strong! Hold strong!' whispered a voice in her mind.

'Pull, girl, pull!' whispered another.

And then a voice that sounded like her mother's – her own mother, her real, wonderful, maddening, infuriating, glorious mother, just said, 'Well done, Coraline,' and that was enough.

The door started to slip closed, easily as anything.

'No!' screamed a voice from beyond the door, and it no longer sounded even faintly human.

Something snatched at Coraline, reaching through the closing gap between the door and the doorpost. Coraline jerked her head out of the way, but the door began to open once more.

'We're going to go home,' said Coraline. 'We are. Help me.' She ducked the snatching fingers.

They moved through her, then: ghost-hands lent her strength that she no longer possessed. There was a final moment of resistance, as if something were caught in the door, and then, with a crash, the wooden door banged closed.

Something dropped from Coraline's head height to the floor. It landed with a sort of a scuttling thump.

'Come on!' said the cat. 'This is not a good place to be in. Quickly.'

Coraline turned her back on the door and began to run, as fast as was practical, through the dark corridor, dragging her hand along the wall to make sure she didn't bump into anything or get turned around in the darkness.

It was an uphill run, and it seemed to her that it went on for a longer distance than anything could possibly go. The wall she was touching seemed warm and yielding now, and, she realised, it felt as if it was covered in a fine downy fur. It moved, as if it were taking a breath. She snatched her hand away from it.

Winds howled in the dark.

She was scared she would bump into something, and she put out her hand for the wall once more. This time what she touched felt hot and wet, as if she had put her hand in somebody's mouth, and she pulled it back with a small wail.

Her eyes had adjusted to the dark. She could half see, as faintly glowing patches ahead of her, two adults, three children. She could hear the cat, too, padding in the dark in front of her.

And there was something else, which suddenly scuttled between her feet, nearly sending Coraline flying. She caught herself before she went down, using her own momentum to keep moving. She knew that if she fell in that corridor she might never get up again. Whatever that corridor was was older by far than the other mother. It was deep, and slow, and it knew that she was there . . .

Then daylight appeared, and she ran towards it, puffing and wheezing. 'Almost there,' she called encouragingly, but in the light she discovered that the wraiths had gone, and she was alone. She did not have time to wonder what had happened to them. Panting for breath, she staggered through the door and slammed it behind her with the loudest, most satisfying bang you can imagine.

Coraline locked the door with the key, and put the key back into her pocket.

The black cat was huddled in the farthest corner of the room, the pink tip of its tongue showing, its eyes wide. Coraline went over to it, and crouched down.

'I'm sorry,' she said. 'I'm sorry I threw you at her. But it was the only way to distract her enough to get us all out. She would never have kept her word, would she?'

The cat looked up at her, then it rested its head on her hand, licking her fingers with its sandpapery tongue. It began to purr.

'Then we're friends?' said Coraline.

She sat down on one of her grandmother's uncomfortable armchairs, and the cat sprang up into her lap and made itself comfortable. The light that came through the picture window was daylight, real golden late-afternoon daylight, not a white mist-light. The sky was a robin's-egg blue, and Coraline could see trees and, beyond the trees, green hills, which faded on the horizon into purples and greys. The sky had never seemed so *sky*; the world had never seemed so *world*.

Coraline stared at the leaves on the trees and at the patterns of light and shadow on the cracked bark of the trunk of the beech tree outside the window, then she looked down at her lap, at the way that the rich sunlight brushed every hair on the cat's head, turning each white whisker to gold.

Nothing, she thought, had ever been so *interesting*.

And, caught up in the interestingness of the world, Coraline barely noticed that she had wriggled down and curled, cat-like, in her grandmother's uncomfortable armchair, nor did she notice when she fell into a deep and dreamless sleep.

The pale girl fluttered a little over their heads,
swooping down on butterfly wings to grab the ball . . .

CHAPTER 12

Her mother shook her gently awake.

'Coraline?' she said. 'Darling, what a funny place to fall asleep. And really, this room is only for best. We looked all over the house for you.'

Coraline stretched and blinked. 'I'm sorry,' she said. 'I fell asleep.'

'I can see that,' said her mother. 'And wherever did the cat come from? He was waiting by the front door when I came in. Shot out like a bullet as I opened it.'

'Probably had things to do,' said Coraline. Then she hugged her mother, so tightly that her arms began to ache. Her mother hugged Coraline back.

'Dinner in fifteen minutes,' said her mother. 'Don't forget to wash your hands. And just *look* at those pyjama bottoms. What did you do to your poor knee?'

'I tripped,' said Coraline. She went into the

bathroom, and she washed her hands and cleaned her bloody knee. She put ointment on her cuts and scrapes.

She went into her bedroom – her real bedroom, her true bedroom. She pushed her hands into the pockets of her dressing gown, and she pulled out three marbles, a stone with a hole in it, the black key, and an empty snow-globe.

She shook the snow-globe and watched the glittery snow swirl through the water to fill the empty world. She put it down and watched the snow fall, covering the place where the little couple had once stood.

Coraline took a piece of string from her toybox and she strung the black key on to it. Then she knotted the string and hung it around her neck.

'There,' she said. She put on some clothes, and hid the key under her T-shirt. It was cold against her skin. The stone went into her pocket.

Coraline walked down the hallway to her father's study. He had his back to her, but she knew, just on seeing him, that his eyes, when he turned around, would be her father's kind grey eyes, and she crept over and kissed him on the back of his balding head.

'Hello, Coraline,' he said. Then he looked round and smiled at her. 'What was that for?'

'Nothing,' said Coraline. 'I just miss you some-times. That's all.'

'Oh good,' he said. He put the computer to sleep, stood up, and then, for no reason at all, he picked Coraline up, which he had not done for such a long time, not since he had started pointing out to her she was much too old to be carried, and he carried her into the kitchen.

Dinner that night was pizza, and even though it was home-made by her father (so the crust was alternately thick and doughy and raw, or too thin and burnt), and even though he had put slices of green pepper on it, along with little meatballs and, of all things, pineapple chunks, Coraline ate the entire slice she had been given.

Well, she ate everything except for the pineapple chunks.

And soon enough it was bedtime.

Coraline kept the key around her neck, but she put the grey marbles beneath her pillow; and in bed that night, Coraline dreamed a dream.

She was at a picnic, under an old oak tree, in a green meadow. The sun was high in the sky and, while there were distant fluffy white clouds on the horizon, the sky above her head was a deep, untroubled blue.

There was a white-linen cloth laid on the grass, with bowls piled high with food – she could see salads and sandwiches, nuts and fruit, jugs of lemonade and water and thick chocolate milk. Coraline sat on one side of the tablecloth while three other children took a side each. They were dressed in the oddest clothes.

The smallest of them, sitting on Coraline's left, was a boy with red-velvet knee-britches and a frilly white shirt. His face was dirty, and he was piling his plate high with boiled new potatoes and with what looked like cold, whole, cooked trout. 'This is the finest of picnics, lady,' he said to her.

'Yes,' said Coraline. 'I think it is. I wonder who organised it.'

'Why, I rather think you did, miss,' said a tall girl, sitting opposite Coraline. She wore a brown, rather shapeless dress, and had a brown bonnet on her head which tied beneath her chin. 'And we are more grateful for it and for all than ever words can say.' She was eating slices of bread and jam, deftly cutting the bread from a large golden-brown loaf with a huge knife, then spooning on the purple jam with a wooden spoon. She had jam all around her mouth.

'Aye. This is the finest food I have eaten in centuries,' said the girl on Coraline's right. She was a very pale child, dressed in what seemed to be spiders' webs, with a circle of glittering silver set in her blonde hair. Coraline could have sworn that the girl had two wings – like dusty silver butterfly wings, not bird wings – coming out of her back.

The girl's plate was piled high with pretty flowers. She smiled at Coraline, as if it had been a very long time since she had smiled and she had almost, but not quite, forgotten how. Coraline found herself liking this girl immensely.

And then, in the way of dreams, the picnic had ended and they were playing in the meadow, running and shouting and tossing a glittering ball from one to another. Coraline knew it was a dream then, because none of them ever got tired or winded or out of breath. She wasn't even sweating. They just laughed and ran in a game that was partly tag, partly piggy-in-the-middle, and partly just a magnificent romp.

Three of them ran along the ground, while the pale girl fluttered a little over their heads, swooping down on butterfly wings to grab the ball and swinging up again into the sky before she tossed the ball to one of the other children.

And then, without a word about it being spoken, the game was over and the four of them went back to the picnic cloth, where the lunch had been cleared away, and there were four bowls waiting for them, three of ice-cream, one of honeysuckle flowers piled high.

They ate with relish.

'Thank you for coming to my party,' said Coraline. 'If it is mine.'

'The pleasure is ours, Coraline Jones,' said the winged girl, nibbling another honeysuckle blossom. 'If there were but something we could do for you, to thank you, and to reward you.'

'Aye,' said the boy with the red-velvet britches and the dirty face. He put out his hand and held Coraline's hand with his own. It was warm now.

'It's a very fine thing you did for us, miss,' said the tall girl. She now had a smear of chocolate ice-cream all around her lips.

'I'm just pleased it's all over,' said Coraline.

Was it her imagination, or did a shadow cross the faces of the other children at the picnic?

The winged girl, the circlet in her hair glittering like a star, rested her fingers for a moment on the back of Coraline's hand. 'It is over and done with for *us*,' she said. 'This is our staging post. From here, we three will set out for uncharted lands, and what comes after no one alive can say . . .' She stopped talking.

'There's a *but*, isn't there?' said Coraline. 'I can feel it. Like a rain cloud.'

The boy on her left tried to smile bravely, but his lower lip began to tremble and he bit it with his upper teeth and said nothing. The girl in the brown bonnet shifted uncomfortably and said, 'Yes, miss.'

'But I got you three back,' said Coraline. 'I got Mum and Dad back. I shut the door. I locked it. What more was I meant to do?'

The boy squeezed Coraline's hand with his. She found herself remembering when it had been her, trying to reassure him, when he was little more than a cold memory in the darkness.

'Well, can't you give me a clue?' asked Coraline. 'Isn't there *something* you can tell me?'

'The beldam swore by her good right hand,' said the tall girl, 'but she lied.'

'M-my governess,' said the boy, 'used to say that nobody is ever given more to shoulder than he or she can bear.' He shrugged as he said this, as if he had not yet made his own mind up whether or not it was true.

'We wish you luck,' said the winged girl. 'Good fortune and wisdom and courage – although you have already shown that you have all three of these blessings, and in abundance.'

'She hates you,' blurted out the boy. 'She hasn't lost anything for so long. Be wise. Be brave. Be tricky.'

'But it's not *fair*,' said Coraline, in her dream, angrily. 'It's just not *fair*. It should be over.'

The boy with the dirty face stood up and hugged Coraline tightly. 'Take comfort in this,' he whispered. 'Th'art alive. Thou livest.'

And in her dream Coraline saw that the sun had set and the stars were twinkling in the darkening sky.

Coraline stood in the meadow, and she watched as the three children (two of them walking, one flying) went away from her, across the grass, silver in the light of the huge moon.

The three of them came to a small wooden bridge over a stream. They stopped there, and turned and waved, and Coraline waved back.

And what came after was darkness.

Coraline woke in the early hours of the morning, convinced she had heard something moving, but unsure what it was.

She waited.

Something made a rustling noise outside her bedroom door. She wondered if it was a rat. The door rattled. Coraline clambered out of bed.

'Go away,' said Coraline, sharply. 'Go away or you'll be sorry.'

There was a pause, then the whatever-it-was scuttled away down the hall. There was something odd and irregular about its footsteps, if they *were* footsteps. Coraline found herself wondering if it was perhaps a rat with an extra leg . . .

'It isn't over, is it?' she said to herself.

Then she opened the bedroom door. The grey, pre-dawn light showed her the whole of the corridor, completely deserted.

She went towards the front door, sparing a hasty

glance back at the wardrobe-door mirror hanging on the wall at the other end of the hallway, seeing nothing but her own pale face staring back at her, looking sleepy and serious. Gentle, reassuring snores came from her parents' room, but the door was closed. All the doors off the corridor were closed. Whatever the scuttling thing was, it had to be here somewhere.

Coraline opened the front door and looked at the grey sky. She wondered how long it would be until the sun came up, wondered whether her dream had been a true thing while knowing in her heart that it had been. Something she had taken to be part of the shadows under the hall couch detached itself from beneath the couch and made a mad, scrabbling rush on its long white legs, heading for the front door.

Coraline's mouth dropped open in horror and she stepped out of the way as the thing clicked and scuttled past her and out of the house, running crablike on its too-many tapping, clicking, scurrying feet.

She knew what it was, and she knew what it was after. She had seen it too many times in the last few days, reaching and clutching and snatching and popping black beetles obediently into the other mother's mouth. Five-footed, crimson-nailed, the colour of bone.

It was the other mother's right hand.

It wanted the black key.

It made one triumphant, nail-clacking leap
on to the centre of the paper tablecloth.

CHAPTER 13

Coraline's parents never seemed to remember anything about their time in the snow-globe. At least, they never said anything about it, and Coraline never mentioned it to them.

Sometimes, she wondered whether they had ever noticed that they had lost two days in the real world, and came to the eventual conclusion that they had not. Then again, there are some people who keep track of every day and every hour, and there are people who don't, and Coraline's parents were solidly in the second camp.

Coraline had placed the marbles beneath her pillow before she went to sleep that first night home in her own room once more. She went back to bed, after she saw the other mother's hand, although there was not much time left for sleeping, and she rested her head back on the pillow.

Something scrunched gently as she did so.

She sat up and lifted the pillow. The fragments of the glass marbles that she saw looked like the remains of eggshells one finds beneath trees in springtime: like empty, broken robins' eggs, or even more delicate, wrens' eggs, perhaps.

Whatever had been inside the glass spheres had gone. Coraline thought of the three children waving goodbye to her in the moonlight, waving before they crossed that silver stream.

She gathered up the eggshell-thin fragments with care and placed them in a small blue box which had once held a bracelet that her grandmother had given her when she was a little girl. The bracelet was long-lost, but the box remained.

Miss Spink and Miss Forcible came back from visiting Miss Spink's niece, and Coraline went down to their flat for tea. It was a Monday. On Wednesday Coraline would go back to school: a whole new school year would begin.

Miss Forcible insisted on reading Coraline's tea leaves.

'Well, looks like everything's mostly shipshape and Bristol fashion, lovey,' said Miss Forcible.

'Sorry?' said Coraline.

'Everything is coming up roses,' said Miss Forcible. 'Well, almost everything. I'm not sure what *that* is.' She pointed to a clump of tea leaves sticking to the side of the cup.

Miss Spink tutted and reached for the cup. 'Honestly, Miriam. Give it over here. Let me see . . .'

She blinked through her thick spectacles. 'Oh dear. No, I have no idea what that signifies. It looks almost like a hand.'

Coraline looked. The clump of leaves did look a little like a hand, reaching for something.

Hamish the Scottie dog was hiding under Miss Forcible's chair, and he wouldn't come out.

'I think he was in some sort of fight,' said Miss Spink. 'He has a deep gash in his side, poor dear. We'll take him to the vet later this afternoon. I wish I knew what could have done it.'

Something, Coraline knew, would have to be done.

That final week of the holidays, the weather was magnificent, as if the summer itself were trying to make up for the miserable weather they had been having by giving them some bright and glorious days before it ended.

The crazy old man upstairs called down to Coraline when he saw her coming out of Miss Spink and Miss Forcible's flat.

'Hey! Hi! You! Caroline!' he shouted over the railing.

'It's Coraline,' she said. 'How are the mice?'

'Something has frightened them,' said the old man, scratching his moustache. 'I think maybe there is a weasel in the house. Something is about. I heard it in the night. In my country we would have put down a trap for it, maybe put down a little meat or hamburger, and when the creature comes to feast, then – bam! – it would be caught and never bother us more. The mice are so scared they will not even pick up their little musical instruments.'

'I don't think it wants meat,' said Coraline. She put her hand up and touched the black key that hung about her neck. Then she went inside.

She bathed herself, and kept the key round her neck the whole time she was in the bath. She never took it off any more.

Something scratched at her bedroom window after she went to bed. Coraline was almost asleep, but she slipped out of bed and pulled open the curtains. A white hand with crimson fingernails leapt from the window-ledge on to a drainpipe and was immediately out of sight. There were deep gouges in the glass on the other side of the window.

Coraline slept uneasily that night, waking from time to time to plot and plan and ponder, then falling back into sleep, never quite certain where her pondering ended and the dream began, one ear always open for the sound of something scratching at her windowpane or at her bedroom door.

In the morning Coraline said to her mother, 'I'm going to have a picnic with my dolls today. Can I borrow a sheet – an old one, one you don't need any longer – as a tablecloth?'

'I don't think we have one of those,' said her mother. She opened the kitchen drawer that held the napkins and the tablecloths, and she prodded about in it. 'Hold on. Will this do?'

It was a folded-up disposable paper tablecloth covered with red flowers, left over from some picnic they had been on several years before.

'That's perfect,' said Coraline.

'I didn't think you played with your dolls any more,' said Mrs Jones.

'I don't,' admitted Coraline. 'They're protective coloration.'

'Well, be back in time for lunch,' said her mother. 'Have a good time.'

Coraline filled a cardboard box with dolls and several plastic dolls' teacups. She filled a jug with water.

Then she went outside. She walked down to the road, just as if she were going to the shops. Before she reached the supermarket she cut over a fence into some wasteland, and along an old drive, then she crawled under a hedge. She had to go under the hedge in two journeys in order not to spill the water from the jug.

It was a long, roundabout looping journey, but at the end of it Coraline was satisfied that she had not been followed.

She came out behind the dilapidated old tennis court. She crossed over it to the meadow where the long grass swayed. She found the planks on the edge of the meadow. They were astonishingly heavy – almost too heavy for a girl to lift, even using all her strength, but she managed. She didn't have any choice. She pulled the planks out of the way, one by one, grunting and sweating with the effort, revealing a deep, round, brick-lined hole in the ground. It smelled of damp and the dark. The bricks were greenish and slippery.

She spread out the tablecloth and laid it carefully over the top of the well. She put a plastic dolls' cup every twenty centimetres or so, at the edge of the well, and she weighed each cup down with water from the jug.

She put a doll in the grass beside each cup, making it look as much like a dolls' tea party as she could. Then she retraced her steps, back under the hedge, along the dusty yellow drive, around the back of the shops, back to her house.

She reached up and took the key from around her neck. She dangled it from the string, as if the key were just something she liked to play with. Then she knocked on the door of Miss Spink and Miss Forcible's flat.

Miss Spink opened the door.

'Hello, dear,' she said.

'I don't want to come in,' said Coraline. 'I just wanted to find out how Hamish was doing.'

Miss Spink sighed. 'The vet says that Hamish is a brave little soldier,' she said. 'Luckily, the cut doesn't seem to be infected. We cannot imagine what could have done it. The vet says some animal, he thinks, but has no idea what. Mister Bobo says he thinks it might have been a weasel.'

'Mister Bobo?'

'The man in the top flat. Mister Bobo. Fine old circus family I believe. Romanian or Slovenian or Livonian, or one of those countries. Bless me, I can never remember them any more.'

It had never occurred to Coraline that the crazy old man upstairs actually had a name, she realised. If she'd known his name was Mr Bobo she would have said it every chance she got. How often do you get to say a name like 'Mister Bobo' aloud?

'Oh,' said Coraline to Miss Spink. 'Mister Bobo.

Right. Well,' she said, a little louder, 'I'm going to go and play with my dolls now, over by the old tennis court, round the back.'

'That's nice, dear,' said Miss Spink. Then she added, confidentially, 'Make sure you keep an eye out for the old well. Mister Lovat, who was here before your time, said that he thought it might go down for half a mile or more.'

Coraline hoped that the hand had not heard this last remark, and she changed the subject. 'This key?' said Coraline, loudly. 'Oh, it's just some old key from our house. It's part of my game. That's why I'm carrying it around with me on this piece of string. Well, goodbye now.'

'What an extraordinary child,' said Miss Spink to herself as she closed the door.

Coraline ambled across the meadow towards the old tennis court, dangling and swinging the black key on its piece of string as she walked.

Several times she thought she saw something the colour of bone in the undergrowth. It was keeping pace with her, about ten metres away.

She tried to whistle, but nothing happened, so she sang out loud instead, a song her father had made up for her when she was a little baby and which had always made her laugh. It went:

Oh . . . My twitchy witchy girl
I think you are so nice,
I give you bowls of porridge
And I give you bowls of ice-
cream.
I give you lots of kisses,
And I give you lots of hugs,
But I never give you sandwiches
with bugs
in.

That was what she sang as she sauntered through the woods, and her voice hardly trembled at all.

The dolls' tea party was where she had left it. She was relieved that it was not a windy day, for everything was still in its place, every water-filled plastic cup weighed down the paper tablecloth as it was meant to. She breathed a sigh of relief.

Now was the hardest part.

'Hello, dolls,' she said brightly. 'It's teatime!'

She walked close to the paper tablecloth. 'I brought the lucky key,' she told the dolls. 'To make sure we have a good picnic.'

And then, as carefully as she could, she leaned over and gently placed the key on the tablecloth. She was still holding on to the string. She held her breath, hoping that the cups of water at the edges of the well would weigh the cloth down, letting it take the weight of the key without collapsing into the well.

The key sat in the middle of the paper picnic cloth. Coraline let go of the string and took a step back. Now it was all up to the hand.

She turned to her dolls.

'Who would like a piece of cherry cake?' she asked. 'Jemima? Pinky? Primrose?' and she served each doll a slice of invisible cake on an invisible plate, chattering happily as she did so.

From the corner of her eye she saw something bone white scamper from one tree trunk to another, closer and closer. She forced herself not to look at it.

'Jemima!' said Coraline. 'What a bad girl you are! You've dropped your cake! Now I'll have to go over and get you a whole new slice!' And she walked around the tea party until she was on the other side of it to the hand. She pretended to clean up spilled cake and then to get Jemima another piece.

And then, in a skittering, chittering rush, it came. The hand, running high on its fingertips, scrabbled through the tall grass and up on to a tree stump. It stood there for a moment, like a crab tasting the air, and then it made one triumphant, nail-clacking leap on to the centre of the paper tablecloth.

Time slowed for Coraline. The white fingers closed around the black key . . .

And then the weight and the momentum of the hand sent the plastic dolls' cups flying, and the paper tablecloth and the key and the other mother's right hand went tumbling down into the darkness of the well.

Coraline counted slowly under her breath. She got up to forty before she heard a muffled splash coming from a long way below.

Someone had once told her that if you look up at the sky from the bottom of a mineshaft, even in the brightest daylight, you see a night sky and stars. Coraline wondered if the hand could see stars from where it was.

She hauled the heavy planks back on to the well, covering it as carefully as she could. She didn't want anything to fall in. She didn't want anything ever to get out. Then she put her dolls and the cups back in the cardboard box she had carried them out in. Something caught her eye while she was doing this, and she straightened up in time to see the black cat stalking towards her, its tail held high and curling at the tip like a question mark. It was the first time she had seen the cat in several days, since they had returned together from the other mother's place.

The cat walked over to her and jumped up on to the planks that covered the well. Then, slowly, it winked one eye at her.

It sprang down into the long grass in front of her and rolled over on to its back, wiggling about ecstatically.

Coraline scratched and tickled the soft fur on its belly, and the cat purred contentedly. When it had had enough it rolled over on to its front once more and walked back towards the tennis court, like a tiny patch of midnight in the midday sun.

Coraline went back to the house.

Mr Bobo was waiting for her in the driveway. He clapped her on the shoulder.

'The mice tell me that all is good,' he said. 'They say that you are our saviour, Caroline.'

'It's Coraline, Mister Bobo,' said Coraline. 'Not Caroline. Coraline.'

'Coraline,' said Mr Bobo, repeating her name to himself with wonderment and respect. 'Very good, Coraline. The mice say that I must tell you that as soon as they are ready to perform in public, you will come up to watch them as the first audience of all. They will play *tumpty umpty* and *toodle oodle*, and they will dance and do a thousand tricks. That is what they say.'

'I would like that very much,' said Coraline. 'When they're ready.'

She knocked at Miss Spink and Miss Forcible's door. Miss Spink let her in and Coraline went into their parlour. She put her box of dolls down on the floor. Then she put her hand into her pocket and pulled out the stone with the hole in it.

'Here you go,' she said. 'I don't need it any more. I'm very grateful. I think it may have saved my life, and saved some other people's deaths.'

She gave them both tight hugs, although her arms barely stretched around Miss Spink, and Miss Forcible smelled like the raw garlic she had been cutting. Then Coraline picked up her box of dolls and went out.

'What an extraordinary child,' said Miss Spink. No one had hugged her like that since she had retired from the theatre.

That night Coraline lay in bed, all bathed, teeth cleaned, with her eyes open, staring up at the ceiling.

It was warm enough that, now the hand was gone, she had opened her bedroom window wide. She had insisted to her father that the curtains not be entirely closed.

Her new school clothes were laid out carefully on her chair for her to put on when she woke.

Normally, on the night before the first day of term, Coraline was apprehensive and nervous. But, she realised, there was nothing left about school that could scare her any more.

She fancied she could hear sweet music on the night air: the kind of music that can only be played on the tiniest silver trombones and trumpets and bassoons, on piccolos and tubas so delicate and small that their keys could only be pressed by the tiny pink fingers of white mice.

Coraline imagined that she was back again in her dream, with the two girls and the boy under the oak tree in the meadow, and she smiled.

As the first stars came out Coraline finally allowed herself to drift into sleep, while the gentle upstairs music of the mouse circus spilled out on to the warm evening air, telling the world that the summer was almost over.